THOMAS J. [   ]E

CAST THE
FIRST STONE

ARTWORK BY SUE MASSEY

CAST THE FIRST STONE
(Mark Mason #1)
THOMAS J. STONE ©2020

COVER ARTWORK BY SUE MASSEY

Saturday April 18th

Mark Mason woke with a start. He hadn't got to sleep until around 2am because he'd really lost track of time while reading. It was almost 11am and now he was far behind in his normal Saturday routine. Luckily it was the weekend and he didn't need to go to the office where he felt like a battery hen in his little cubicle. Selling third rate mobile phone contracts was not what he wanted from a career but needs must at the moment. He had bills to pay. He knew his parents would help him out but pride and a determination to make his own way in the world overcame any thought of charity.

After a quick breakfast of cereal and orange juice he got ready for his visit to the gym followed by a 3 or 4 mile walk to relax and warm down. Before leaving he looked in the mirror and ruffled his thick, blond hair. No point in trying to comb it with the stuff he'd put in it before his night out with a couple of friends. He was bemused that people actually spent money to get a scruffy haircut when he was getting it for free every day. Mark was of average height with a decent build, willowy would be the word he'd describe himself as. Not like the muscle bound roid heads he sometimes saw at the gym lifting weights heavier than he was. If he tried to do that he'd cripple himself. He'd torn a disc in his back about four years previously in a car crash. Until then he'd been very active playing football and cricket and a lot of jogging to keep himself fit. He drove to the gym in his old Jaguar and spent the next hour doing some tiny toning weights, some stretching and 40 minutes on the static bike. He preferred to walk these days though. Relaxation was always a part of his routine.

He got home just about 1pm and put his Bluetooth earbuds into his ears and started off his pedometer and music player on his phone. Immediately Thin Lizzy blared into his head. Although he was only 27 he loved Classic Rock and most of his favourite bands came from the 70s and 80s. It was real music made by real musicians and not the modern rubbish of just a catchy repetitive phrase that put people in a trance.

It was early April and the weather had been fine for about a week so he decided he'd take his first walk over the farmer's fields not far away. He had a quick stretch as his back often got a little stiff while driving and made his way up the hill from his house. On the way he waved at his neighbour Steve Jones who was tackling his front lawn with his shiny new orange hover mower. Steve stopped the mower and walked over to Mark. He was quite tall and lean with short dark hair and a ready smile. He wore what he called his 'gardening togs' which were an old purple sweatshirt and camouflage trousers and ancient brown work boots. People just couldn't help liking Steve and his friendly manner.

"Finally got some decent weather for a change. You off on your walk mate?"

"About time the weather cleared up. I've been looking forward to getting over the fields for weeks. Hopefully it's nice and dry over there and no mud," replied Mark.

"I heard we're in for a hot summer this year. Seems the winters are shorter these days, maybe this climate change has it's advantages."

"Yeah, I should get a few ten milers in over the summer. It would be easier and quicker if I could have a jog but you know how my back is mate."

"You wait until you hit forty and everything starts to go downhill, your nose and ears get bigger but some parts seem to get smaller," joked Steve. "All this gardening and DIY I'm forced to do keeps me in shape. Don't get much help from the two boys either."

"You'd only spend the time in the pub watching your rubbish team getting battered every week."

"Good point Mark, we're bloody awful this year but far from relegation candidates, we may even scrape a place in that Micky Mouse European competition for next season."

"You wish. Better get on before I seize up. You up for a beer later?" asked Mark.

"Come over to mine and bring young Nat with you unless she's off clubbing with her mates, she's nicer to look at than you and good company for Kim."

"Will do mate, I'll give her a call after she's finished work."

Steve powered up the electric mower again and rolled his eyes at Mark to emphasise the hopelessness of being consigned to a summer of mowing and weeding over the coming months while Mark carried on up the short gravel hill to the garages where the public footpath was that would take him into the lush, green countryside and a bit of peace and quiet.

The path was stony and rutted and Mark always made sure he was careful on it as other people had twisted ankles in the past. He'd once tried to get it repaired and ended up being directed between the County Council and the local one repeatedly because no one would admit it was their responsibility so he gave up. He finally got to the metal gate at the top of the path and passed through. The earth was firm enough to confirm he'd made the right decision to attempt the field walk.

Thin Lizzy had given way to the Grateful Dead and he briefly wondered if the dead were actually grateful and concluded he wouldn't be surprised if they were with all the problems in the world these days. It just wasn't safe even in civilised countries and he was happy that he lived in the relative safety of the countryside in a fairly large Hertfordshire village although the way it had been expanding recently it would soon be considered a small town and would inherit small town problems like higher crime, vandalism and cheap housing full of Chavs. His old infants school had already been lost to the developers and was now an apartment complex with parking underneath the flats. He remembered his first day at his new school and his first teacher and how shy and terrified he was of something so alien to him. Mrs. Cole, a jolly, plump woman in her fifties, put everyone at ease with a story that everyone listened to attentively and then he played and made friends. Some of them still lived in the village but most had moved away and made their way into the big, wide world. A lot of families went back generations in the rural community, including his own on his mum's side of the family. His mum born in the village to parents who were themselves born there and so on as far back as anyone could remember. Mark's mum was compiling a family tree from the church records. Mark was interested to see how far back she could go.

Mark saw that the farmer had ploughed his big field in preparation for planting corn again. Farmers rarely specialised in one line any more and old Charlie grew corn and kale as well as reared beef cattle, pigs and sheep and also had a herd of dairy cows and goats too that provided milk. Mark visited the farm shop every couple of weeks. The produce was expensive compared to the supermarket in the next town but it was worth it just to get the quality. You could guarantee that the fruit and veg hadn't been stuck in a warehouse somewhere for weeks and was always at it's best. The marmalade and jams were to die for too. He sometimes bought a rather nice spicy Bloody Mary tomato sauce as well.

Mark climbed a short incline to another aluminium gate which took him to the bridge over the by-pass near the M25 and into the proper countryside. Large trees and bushes separated each field and as he walked onwards he looked up and saw a kestrel or a kite soaring above him. He loved nature and saw plenty of it on his field walks. The winter months restricted him to plodding away around the streets and the worst part of that was the constant traffic that distracted him and it all got a bit boring. Over the fields he could just relax and switch off and listen to his music as he walked. The solitary walks gave him an opportunity to sing along to his favourite tunes, he wasn't a great singer but a least he didn't scare the cows. He always joked that he could sing like Jimi Hendrix and play guitar like Freddie Mercury and thought it was a shame it wasn't the other way round. He could imagine himself leading the life of a rock star. *Shooting Star* by Bad Company came through the earbuds to remind him it sometimes wasn't a good life after all.

His mind wandered as he meandered along. He'd been contemplating asking Nat to move in with him. They'd been together over ten months and had been on holiday a couple of times and spent a few weekends away. He knew it wasn't exactly the same but it was a start. She already stayed two or three nights a week anyway. Maybe they could talk about it later and come to some sort of a decision, even in principle. She still lived with her mum so it's not like she had to give up her own place and if things didn't work out it wouldn't be the end of the world. He hoped it wouldn't be. Nat was different. He also knew that Nat didn't like living with her mum. She was always down and that brought Nat down too. Nat spent most of her time in her bedroom with her college coursework and listening to music.

He walked the path into the calm world that he loved. No distractions other than looking out for the little presents cows left behind. He could see the herd in the next field and could tell by the length of the grass that they hadn't been let out in this one for months. The path was slightly overgrown which meant that other walkers had avoided the muddy fields over the winter months too. By July there would be a hard brown patch of flat earth stretching across every field. It was all public right of way so the various farmers whose land people crossed couldn't complain. The only thing they were ever concerned about were dogs worrying the sheep and the calves although any dog that tried to attack a calf would end up in a bad way from the protective mother. Mark had seen people panic sometimes when the cows got a little too close to them but he knew they were no real danger and he regularly gave them a pat or a stroke when they came close and even let them lick his hand on occasion. He believed that all animals could sense if they were safe with a particular person and they would feel at ease with him. He was certainly no danger to any of the animals on his walks, he even tried to avoid stepping on insects.

He got to the end of the path and moved through what is called a kissing gate. A metal semi circle with four or six horizontal bars where you entered one end and then swung the gate part behind you so you could exit the other side. They had largely replaced wooden stiles over the years and they lasted for years before they got a spot of rust and did not rot away like wood and no climbing over wet wooden steps covered in mud. He wondered if city kids had ever seen one and felt sorry for them that they could potentially spend their entire life in a city full of high rise buildings, manically busy roads and a level of crime that would appal people in rural areas. They would only see animals, apart from cats and dogs and probably rats, at a zoo but you couldn't really call that wildlife. Maybe they loved that sort of life but there was no way Mark could ever live in a city like London or Manchester. He'd be the proverbial fish out of water and would hate it.

He was through the gate and could immediately see the cows had been busy doing their thing so was extra careful on the path as he was wearing his new walking trainers and really didn't want to put them in the washing machine this early. The Friesian cows ignored him for a change, concentrating on filling their stomachs with the juicy eight inch long grass still moist even after a week of no rain. He moved through the large herd, only a couple of times did he need to stray from the path to go round one of the cows who refused to move. Easier to go round than try to move one of the big black and white beasts anyway. There was a large irregular shaped pond in the corner of the field near a cluster of elm trees. Mark wondered why the farmer had never had it drained, he probably would have if it was used for crops but this field was always pasture land for as long as he could remember. Three cows were drinking from the pond in the shade of the trees totally ignoring him.

A little further on he was looking into the distance at the lush rolling countryside while approaching another kissing gate, this one a bit older than the galvanised steel and was made of wood, and still pretty sturdy though but would probably be replaced in a couple of years, when he tripped over a tree root that had been exposed over the winter by melting snow and then the torrential rain of late February.

"Shit!" he cursed as he felt the flexor muscle that joins the hip to the top of his thigh tweak. He'd need to get ice on that as soon as he was home. He used the gate post to balance himself and took his weight off his right leg for a few seconds and hoped the sprain wasn't too serious. He put weight on his leg now and was relieved there was only a little pain. It could have been a lot more serious and would have ruined any opportunity he had to get out and be mobile for a few weeks.

Just then he looked down and noticed something between the roots. It was grey and flat and would have been mistaken for a common stone if not for the small protrusions on three of the sides. He squatted down with most of his weight on his good leg and foraged between the dark, scaly roots for the object. It was just out of reach but he cleared some of the damp earth away and just got two fingertips to it and managed to drag it out. He could see that it was indeed made from stone but carved. He wondered just how old it was and would show it to his mum who was a bit of a history buff and would have more idea than him. Considering it had been surrounded by earth and under a tree root it felt slightly warm which was a bit weird. He put it in his pocket and would clean it up later so he could take a better look at it.

He decided not to aggravate his sprain any more and began to amble back home just as Robert Johnson's *Walking Blues* started playing on the phone as if mocking him.

Natalie Cross was at work in the jewellers she'd been at since she left school. She hated the job and her leering, suggestive boss. She couldn't wait for the day when she could complete her Open University course and tell him to stick the job. She was normally a nice, friendly person but nine long years of his endless innuendo had really got to her over the years. She wished she'd had the courage to have left long before now but she didn't want to risk being jobless, especially as her mum was on her own and needed her support. She was always afraid of taking a chance, playing it safe. As it was a Saturday there were two other girls working with her. They didn't seem to get the same attention from her boss that Nat got. Why can't he pick on them for a change? Nat suggested they went for a quick drink before she got the bus to Mark's place.

As soon as Mark got home he stripped and had a hot shower. Normally a time to think, he just closed his mind off and stood in the almost scalding flow, soaping and rinsing himself as if on autopilot. After drying himself he walked naked to the kitchen and found the ice pack pushed to the back of the little freezer section of the fridge, went back to the bedroom and lay on the bed with the ice pack covering the top of his thigh. He used the remote for the stereo to start off a CD with light classical music and lay back and closed his eyes and dozed for a couple of hours. He was woken by the phone on the bedside cabinet and answered on the fifth ring.

"Hello?" he said, still not quite awake.

"Hi babe, it's me," bubbled Natalie, "I've just finished work and going for a couple of drinks with the girls. Should be there about seven."

"No problem. Steve asked us round for a drink later so can you pick up a takeaway on your way back and we'll eat before we nip over."

"Chinese?" said Nat hoping that Mark was in an oriental mood instead of the normal curry or pizza one."

"Sounds great, I do fancy some of their Hot & Sour soup and pancake rolls. I'll have the plates ready. See you later Pixie."

After they both hung up he remembered the stone from under the tree roots. It must still be in one of the pockets of his jogging bottoms with his phone as he didn't even bother to empty them before showering. He found the bottoms just inside the bathroom door, one leg showing the faint wet imprint of one of his feet he must have left as he got out of the shower, dry now but still showing the residue of the soap from the bottom of the stall.

He retrieved his phone and the three inch by two mud covered carved mystery and walked the few steps to the sink, put his phone on the window sill and turned the hot water tap on and let the water flow onto the stone he'd placed in the basin while he turned to hunt for the nail brush on the small shelf to his right. Finding it underneath a pack of Nat's make up removing wipes he returned to the sink where he saw that the hot water had already removed a little of the mud and a thin trail of silt was disappearing down the plug hole. Mark picked up the stone again and started to gently scrub with the brush and more and more of the dirt was coming off it and exposing an ornate carved surface that looked like flames to him. He was starting to reveal an inscription around the outside of it too but he couldn't read the intricate lettering, it looked like Runic symbols to his untrained eye but he'd seen enough of the medieval language on documentaries to recognise it. He turned it over and more of the mud came away from the surface and looked into a pair of intense eyes staring back at him. He though that this may be the front of the object and the runes were on the rear. The face belonged to what looked like a clown or a jester with a long chin and razor sharp nose and a smile that would have scared a heavyweight boxer let alone children.

"No wonder someone buried you mate," he said under his breath. He needed a thinner implement to remove the dirt from the fine etching of the piece and picked up the old toothbrush from the pot on the window sill that he used to clean the taps and other chrome in the bathroom when he felt like it. He wasn't the most house proud man on the planet. Maybe he needed someone to come in and do it all for him. He couldn't afford a professional cleaner on his wages though so he'd have to do it as and when he found the time. The toothbrush was doing a good job of getting into the tiny crevices of the article in his hand but it was slow going to get all the debris out of the tiny grooves that made up the lettering and the features of the less than handsome face. He found his mind wandering while he worked and wondered just who had buried the stone or was it just lost by accident? The possibilities were endless and he was intrigued about the history of the thing now.

The front door opened and Nat almost staggered in holding a couple of brown paper carrier bags from the Chinese. She looked beautiful framed in the doorway. Raven haired like a modern Cleopatra with eyes to match and a perfect body. Sometimes it hurt just to look at her perfection. She wore her work clothes, a thin dark grey skirt and a pale blue blouse with the logo of the jewellers she worked at above a small pocket on the left of her chest. It can't be easy on the bus laden with the takeaway he thought. Most days he would pick her up but Saturday was always when he tried to get a few things done, like the gym and the walk, and usually didn't have enough hours in the day.

"Is that a toothbrush in your hand or are you pleased to see me?" she laughed and he realised he was still naked and had apparently been cleaning his find for a couple of hours. Mark couldn't believe how long he'd been absorbed with the stone amulet.

"How was your walk, weren't you going across the fields today?"

"Had to cut it short, tripped over a bloody tree and strained something so hobbled back. I did find this though." He held up the delicate carving and then gave her a quick welcome home kiss. She took the stone from him for a closer look.

"I'll just get dressed quickly before we eat, sorry nothing is ready. Time just got away from me."

"It's OK, it'll only take me a minute. Where abouts did you find it?"

"At the end of the second field after the bridge, just before the old wooden gate. I was looking off into the next field see if the sheep were out and wasn't paying attention to where I was putting my feet."

"That will teach you," giggled Nat. "How's the strain now?"

"Not too bad, I had a hot shower and then put an ice pack on it, should be fine by tomorrow. Still up for lunch at my folk's?"

"Of course. I've got a couple of books your mum wanted to borrow."

"More Historical Romances?"

"What else? You know she loves them. Debauchery and death with a bit of conspiracy all rolled in one. It's a popular genre."
"Obviously," he laughed. "Not my cup of tea though."

Mark was dressed in jeans and a cheesecloth shirt that made him look like a refugee from the seventies. He always said he was born in the wrong decade. All he needed was the shoulder length hair and the denim waistcoat with the Alice Cooper patches on it to complete the picture.

They sat at the kitchen table and ate the delicious takeaway. The soup was gorgeous as usual and it was the only time Mark would eat tofu willingly. He looked at the small, round clock on the wall above the back door and thought they needed to make a move to Steve and Kim's soon. It should be a good night - they usually were at Steve's.

It was just after eight when Mark and Nat crossed the road and walked a little up the hill to Steve's house. It was a medium sized three bedroom with a garden front and back and a path that led to the back garden at the side of the house. A typical ex-council property that Steve got for a song about fifteen years ago. Mark knocked at the front door, admiring the freshly cut lawn and Kim answered and invited them in, planting a kiss on each of them.

"Steve's on the patio with the drinks all ready. I assume you are starting off with the usual?"

"Perfect, Kimmy my dear," replied Mark and walked through the living room to the back of the house and through the sliding double-glazed door onto the patio. Nat held back and she and Kim went to the kitchen.

"Be there in a minute," Nat said and Mark wondered what gossip they were spreading.

"Hi mate, at last it's warm enough for outside relaxation with a good drink. I've been looking forward to this." Mark picked up the ice cold Stella that was waiting for him, the condensation dripping from the bottle onto a beer mat and downed half of it.

"Yeah, first of many I hope, but you never know if you'll get snow in June these days," Steve laughed. "I remember when we used to have seasons and you could actually rely on a weather forecast."

"I see you got the front lawn done."

"First job of the year usually takes a while but the new mower is excellent. I got through the grass in no time. A real bargain if it saves me time on a Saturday."

"I'm assuming you were done in time for the 5:30 kick off at the pub?"

"I wish I hadn't - we were spanked at home again. Can't wait for this season to end so we get a few decent players in during the summer."

"It's getting rid of the crap ones that is harder. If they aren't performing no other team will take a chance on them and teams have to sell before they can buy now, it's the economics of the game."

"Thanks for cheering me up, you dick," laughed Steve. "I saw you were back early from your walk. Getting too old for it?"

"I had a slight accident. Tripped over a tree root and tweaked my hip."

"Muppet! Probably looking for those teenage hikers in the tight shorts you see now and again," joked Steve although he did it quietly so the girls didn't hear.

"It would have been worth it if I did," said Mark, half joking. He reached into his pocket and pulled out the stone carving he had found earlier. It looked in a lot better condition now than when he had found it. He passed it to Steve.

"Found this - could be worth a couple of quid to a collector."

"Jesus, he's an ugly bugger," he commented as he looked at the long chinned figure on the face. "Looks like my boss."

"I doubt that bloke was ever up to his armpits in grease and wielding an arc welder like a light sabre." Mark snorted with laughter and took another swig of his drink."

"I don't think Mick ever evolved enough to develop armpits. He's probably Darwin's Missing Link." They both roared at the thought.

"What's the joke you two?" asked Kim. She had a sly look on her face as if she and Nat had formed some sort of conspiracy in the kitchen. Steve passed to stone to Kim.

"We were thinking how much this looks like Mick Smith."

"Way too good looking for a comparison. This guy, I mean." Everyone burst out laughing again. They all knew how much Kim disliked Steve's boss.

"I'm taking it to my mum tomorrow. If she doesn't know what it is I'm sure she can point me in the direction of someone who may do," said Mark.

"How is your mum?" asked Kim.

"Trying to find things to occupy her time since the retirement and local history is one of them, she's going to do a family tree."

"Looks very old," remarked Kim, "Maybe four or five hundred years, possibly even older."

"Maybe its worth millions and I can pay for us all to have a nice holiday somewhere and then buy a big house and a new car?" wished Mark.

"In your dreams, but it would be nice. We could go the the Maldives," replied Steve.

"It's a deal, anything over a million and we're off the the Maldives, can't wait." Mark said with a wink.

"So what were you two conspiring about?" Steve looked at Kim and Nat.

"Oh, nothing much, girl stuff," replied Kim and smiled at Nat.

"Probably planning to get you hitched mate," joked Steve.

"Maybe if there is any money left over from the Maldives," chuckled Mark. He glanced at Nat and frowned. Did he spot a slight trace of disappointment on her face?

There was an awkward silence for a few seconds and then Kim lightened the mood.

"Anyone want some nice warm sausage rolls?"

"Love some," said Mark, relieved that the subject had been changed. He loved Nat but he wasn't even sure he wanted her to move in yet, let alone marriage.

"Let's move into the front room then, it's getting a little chilly." No one was sure if she meant the weather or the atmosphere but as usual, Kimmy saved the day.

A very tall, dark figure plagued Mark's dreams that night. He walked the fields in the swirling fog and always in the distance the black cloaked presence watched him but he could never get close enough to make out any of their features. Every time he thought he was closing in on it the figure seemed to float backwards through the haze. What did they want? Why was it watching him? Did he really want to find out? The impression of a brooding evil invaded his thoughts and he knew that trying to follow the thing would not be a good idea. He turned and tried to make his way home but every time he looked around the entity was always there, always the same distance behind him. He told himself not to panic and he would be safe at home very soon. He began to pick up his pace despite his own advice and could see the path that led to the estate and the safety of his flat. The individual cloaked in darkness was slowly closing on him, it seemed to float across the misty, muddy ground, no visible movement of either arms or legs. People just couldn't do that, he thought.

Just what the hell was that thing? He was almost jogging now as he hurried on down the rutted path. He knew that a stumble now would make it easy for his dark pursuer to catch him. He got to the end of the uneven track and almost sprinted towards the flat, the pain in his back doing it's best to slow him down. He reached his front door and fumbled the keys out of his pocket and it took three attempts to get the key into the Yale lock.

He got the door open and slammed it shut after he was through. Panting hard and with his back pushed against the door he knew he was safe. Nothing could get into his haven. Then he heard a gravelly whisper on the other side of the door.

"Give it back!"

Sunday April 19th

Mark woke in a cold sweat and was breathing in short, sharp puffs with Iron Maiden's *Fear Of the Dark* pounding inside his head. Nat had woken too.

"You alright babe?" she asked, still in the haze of a half-sleep herself.

"Bad dream. I don't think I've had one like that since I was a little kid."

"What was it about?" asked Nat.

"It's fading quickly, all I really remember was a lot of fog and trying to get home. I think someone was following me," he said, shaking slightly. His hair was soaked in perspiration.

"How does breakfast of bacon and eggs sound to make you forget all about it?"

"What time is it?" he asked, still unable to think properly.

"Almost nine. Let me get a quick shower and I'll get things started."

"Thanks Pixie."

"Why do you call me that? It's not like I'm three feet tall."

"Everyone needs a nickname, I think that's a law somewhere," he smiled.

"Don't nicknames have something the do with the Devil? As in Old Nick?"

"That's a common myth. It actually comes from Old English. The word Ekename means additional name and used as a term of endearment and that got slightly elongated to Nekename and then became Nickname."

"I can't work out why you are selling dodgy phone contracts in a call centre with a brain like yours. Seems a total waste to me," she said, frustrated that he never used his full potential.

"It's a mystery to me too. I just can't work out what I want to do with my life and it always seems to be the wrong time and the wrong place. Things just fall into place for some people and I don't think I'm one of them."

"It'll happen one day babe, your giant brain will think of something and you'll be rich and famous."

"I'd like the rich bit but not too sure of the famous part. I don't know how film and rock stars cope with the constant scrutiny every second of their lives," he said.

"Yeah, I'd hate that myself. I'm not sure if all that money is worth it. Ok, you have the cash to do whatever you want but it's not like you can go to the local pub for a quiet meal and it must be hell on their kids too."

"I doubt Alice Cooper's kids were bullied much but wouldn't want to be the offspring of one of those poncy New Romantic singers," he joked. "Go and shower, I'm getting hungry at the thought of that crispy bacon."

"On my way, boss," she said and then stuck her tongue out like an eight-year-old and grinned.

After breakfast they decided to go for a drive before they had to be at Mark's parent's for lunch.

"When will you ever let me drive this beast?" goaded Nat.

"When you're a grown up," he joked back. "You were used to a little one-litre Micra before you sold it and not a three-litre classic feat of British engineering. Maybe one day if you are good," Mark winked.

"Where are we going?" she asked.

"I thought we'd take a walk around the old stones at Marsham. Soak up that mystical atmosphere, chill out a bit."

"Sounds like a plan to me, get that dream out of your head for good, babe."

Marsham was a small village about ten miles away, centuries old. It had a late fifties feel to it now and the high street shops were still mostly run by the same families for three or four generations. The sort of place where you could film a Hammer movie about sinister goings on in a small community with a big secret. They both loved the place. It was quiet and relatively unknown to anyone not fairly local. The best part was the field on the outskirts that was home to a large stone circle and as it was fairly uncharted as far as the general population was concerned and it wasn't a tourist trap like Avebury in Wiltshire. It was always very quiet and peaceful, they hardly ever saw another soul there. Mark parked the Jag about a quarter of a mile away as access to the site was by path through a small copse. Being hidden like that helped the anonymity of the place and it rarely got visitors other than the locals. They both sauntered around the circle, touching each giant granite pillar in turn, feeling the slight electrical charge from the tall stones. Mark wondered if everyone could feel that same tiny buzz from the stones as he felt. He knew Nat did.

"I love this place, so peaceful," said Nat, smiling in the spring sunshine, breathing in the cool air inside the circle.

"I wonder just how long ago they were erected and why."

"Just one of those mysteries that will never be fully explained. Not unless someone builds a time machine and goes back."

"Time travel has always fascinated me since I was a kid. I was always reading books by Bradbury, Wells, Asimov, Wyndham and a few others."

"Even I've heard of most of them," said Nat with an air of satisfaction. She wasn't keen on Science Fiction books but she liked a lot of the films of the genre. Except Event Horizon, that was far too scary for her and her best friend Erika. Mark thought RomComs were scarier.

They continued to stroll around the inside of the circle and then the outside, examining every bump and crevice and inspecting the patterns the lichen made on the surfaces of the great monoliths, it was almost as if they told their own story. There was a chill starting to pervade the air and Nat shivered a little. She was only wearing a thin light blue blouse with a short yellow cardigan over the top. A mist was appearing between the trees that flanked the stones to the east. Mark thought he saw a tall, dark shape somewhere in the cloudy vapour but put it down to his imagination as it was gone as soon as he glimpsed it, remnants of his dream.

"Getting a bit nippy, maybe we should make a move towards mum's coffee machine?" Mark said as he glanced at his watch. "It's about that time."

Nat nodded. They made the distance between the stones and the car in good time and Mark started the vehicle and waited for the engine to heat the cabin before moving off.

"Do you ever have bad dreams Nat?" he asked.

"You mean monsters, vampires and zombies, that sort of stuff?"

"Anything scary really. That mist reminded me of my dream last night. I even imagined I saw a figure in it," he confessed.

"Probably someone walking their dog or a poacher checking his snares."

"More likely than some tree-dwelling monster or even Bigfoot," he chuckled, starting to feel a lot better now the Jag's heaters were pumping in warmer air.

The sun was beginning to poke through the clouds in places so he decided to take the scenic route to his folk's place. The long, winding country lanes were dry and even though it was a Sunday he hadn't seen another car for a long time. At various points along the lane there were gaps in the tall hedge where the farmers entered their fields by either four-wheel drives or tractors and he saw the landscape fall away for miles in the distance. He just couldn't imagine waking up in a concrete jungle like London every day and the only things he saw would be masonry and machinery. And people … lots of people. He would always be a country boy at heart and even big towns scared him slightly, he couldn't live without the open spaces. He supposed that his aversion to crowded spaces cut down on the job opportunities available to him. He just didn't want to be caught in a giant office block. He thought of the Twin Towers in 2001 and inwardly shuddered. Thousands of people trying to escape down forty or fifty flights of stairs with smoke pluming all around them while several of them tripped and were trampled underfoot. Talk about bad dreams, that would be the ultimate nightmare for him. He wanted to take his mind off the thought so reached to the console and turned the CD player on. Rainbow burst out of the speakers. The cascading vocals of Ronnie James Dio complimenting the guitar of the mad genius Richie Blackmore perfectly as they belted out *Man On The Silver Mountain*.

"It really is a beautiful day, looks like we'll get a break in the weather for a few weeks according to the Met Office," commented Nat.

"That's good," said Mark. "I'll try and get out at least a couple of evenings after work this week to make up for my aborted walk yesterday. My hip feels a lot better this morning."

"I may come with you, I could do with a bit of exercise after standing up in that bloody jewellers every day with barely a rest. The other days I'll revise for my course like a good girl, I can't spend all my time with you. I'd never get anything done," she laughed.

Nat was doing an Open University course on Psychology. That was where she saw her future. Helping people with problems instead of trying to sell nine-carat chains to middle aged men with bad halitosis for barely above minimum wage. Mark admired her dedication and determination. At least she knew what she wanted, unlike him. She had a good future ahead of her.

They arrived at the home of Jack and Ellie Mason just before 1pm. It was a late nineteenth century cottage that Jack had owned for almost thirty years since it was passed down to him by his grandfather. Jack had heard the growl and the pulsating music of the Jaguar as Mark was parking and met them at the door and invited them in. He gave Nat a peck on the cheek and all three walked to the spacious kitchen where Ellie was putting the finishing touches to the roast beef, garnishing with garlic and thyme. The rich smell permeated the whole ground floor and Mark's mouth was watering already. Ellie put the tin tray back in the oven for a final five minutes and dropped her padded oven glove and hugged both of the visitors. She was just below medium height, quite petite in fact. She was 53 years old with short blond hair and still pretty and always reminded Nat of Barbara Bel Geddes in the Hitchcock classic Vertigo, secretly in love with James Stewart even though he regarded her as just a friend and confidante. Nat thought that Ellie was secretly in love with Jimmy too. They loved watching films together. Ellie was like the mother she wished hers would be, they had a lot of shared interests unlike her mum who had no interests at all since Nat's dad had left.
"Coffee?" asked Jack as he moved to the machine. "It's pretty fresh and it's that Colombian we all seem to like." Jack was a tall man, 55 years old

and grey headed. He was slim and was wearing his usual casual attire of a blue shirt and brown slacks but still looked smart enough to meet one of his clients. He'd just got back from a round of golf with a few friends - his Sunday ritual.

"Sounds great, it was getting a little chilly on our walk around the stones at Marsham," replied Mark.

"We haven't been up there for a few years, I've always found the place to be quite relaxing," said Ellie. "You know I love my history, that place was always my favourite haunt on a bright summer's day as a teen. I may take a little trip up there soon and see if I can appreciate it as much again."

"Oh, that reminds me," piped up Nat. "I brought over those books you wanted." She handed Ellie a blue carrier bag full of paperbacks.

"Thanks sweetie, there can't be too many historical romances I haven't read yet, I can't believe you still unearth them," said Ellie eyeing the covers of the worn pre-loved books.

"It's amazing what you can pick up in charity shops, and they are a lot cheaper than paying the postage and getting them from the sellers on Amazon."

"How do you remember which ones we've read?"

"I have an app on my phone that keeps track for us," replied Nat. "Makes things so easy, I just scan the barcodes."

"Seems you can get these apps for almost anything these days, I remember when we didn't even have mobiles phones at all, now no one can live without one."

They all sat and chatted in the kitchen while enjoying their coffees for several minutes as the roast beef browned. The smell coming from the oven was incredible. Nat thought Ellie was such a great cook. Nothing was ever bland, she always knew which combinations of herbs and spices worked well together and the vegetables were always cooked to perfection, even if she was experimenting which she often did. She should really write a recipe book full of her creations. Mark and Nat were usually the ones Ellie tried out her latest concoctions on because she knew she would get an honest appraisal from both of them. Of all the parents of the boyfriends she ever had Nat could honestly say she loved Jack and Ellie like they were her own family. Maybe one day they would be. She smiled at the thought. They had accepted her from the very first minute they had met. Even though they had money they had never come across as posh or pretentious. Jack was an accountant with his own company he'd built up after leaving university. Ellie used to work with him until about two years ago when he insisted she retire and start to enjoy herself after bringing up three children. Mark was the eldest but they also had Ann and Ben who were twins five years younger than Mark. They both lived away from home with their partners not far away and were as close as any siblings could get. Nat was an only child and longed for a sister, but it was never to be. Her parents found they could not have any more kids after Nat was born and after that they grew further apart until they divorced when Nat was five and she still lived with her mum. Nat's dad had moved away to Scotland and worked on the oil rigs. She hadn't heard from him in over a year, not even on her recent birthday. She realised that really didn't upset her as much as it might when she was younger, she realised he was making a new life for himself and it just slipped his mind, disappointing but not the end of the world.

The meal was ready. Jack and Mark sat at the dining table while Nat helped Ellie serve the food. The men would do the washing up afterwards while sipping a nice single malt leaving the ladies to natter about the books they had read recently. They were both avid readers and really couldn't understand why people were reading less over the decades, it was a pleasure for both of them and they couldn't imagine life without books.

The beef was excellent, bought from a local butcher in Marsham who worked from a small shop with sawdust on the floor. A real traditional place of business. The joints were always lovely and his sausages were to die for, especially the black pudding and onion and the pork with caramelised onion. Roast potatoes, roast parsnips, broccoli, carrots and giant peas filled the plate and there was a red wine and honey sauce seasoned with dill. It looked amazing and Nat knew she was in for a culinary delight.

They conversed over lunch about varied subjects like the economy, art, music and planned holidays which progressed to dream holidays. Jack and Ellie had had a second honeymoon in the Maldives, a small island called Thudufushi in the South Ari Atoll. Nat cringed when Jack told her how when the plane landed at Male airport you couldn't see any land on either side of the plane as the runway was quite narrow and was appended to the main island so it seemed the plane was landing in the water. He said even he was a bit nervous about that. Once through immigration they had to take a seaplane to the holiday island which was another experience, especially as the seaplane landed about a hundred yards from the shore at a pontoon because of the coral just under the surface. The passengers had to disembark onto the pontoon not far from the still rotating propellers and be picked up by a small boat. Nat decided she would love her own honeymoon there. Maybe one day.

Dessert was a glorious sherry trifle followed by port. Eventually Ellie and Nat retired to the living room to relax and Jack and Mark moved to the kitchen to rinse everything off before putting it all in the large dishwasher. Jack opened a bottle of ten-year-old Laphroaig single malt and the two of them sat at the kitchen table sipping the fiery amber liquid while they talked.

"Isn't it time you proposed to that sweet girl, Mark?"

"We've only been together about ten months."

"It took me about a week before I knew your mum was the right one and I know Natalie is the right girl for you, I can see it in her eyes how much she loves you son."

"I love her to bits but I'm not sure yet if I want to spend the rest of my life with her."

"We'd pay for the wedding too, no financial strain on her mum or you two at all if that worries you. And her dad doesn't look like showing up too soon either - I can even give her away if she'll have me as a sub," Jack grinned.

"I appreciate the offer. Maybe I'll bring the subject up soon. While I remember I've got something to show mum."

"She saw that as soon as you were born," laughed Jack.

Mark grinned.

They moved into the living room and saw the girls were deep in conversation. Mark hoped it wasn't a similar one to the talk he'd just shared with his dad.

"Mum, what do you make of this?" Mark reached into his pocket and brought out the vaguely triangular stone with a hole bored into the top.

"Where did you find this?" Ellie was already interested in it at first sight.

"Tripped on my walk and discovered it mixed up in the roots of a tree," replied Mark.

"It's certainly unusual. I don't think I've ever seen one with three protrusions before and obviously the text around the outside is Runic. Maybe fifteen or sixteen hundred years old. It's definitely some kind of amulet but it's hard to tell if it was used to ward off evil or to attract it without a full translation."

"Do you know anyone who can do it?" asked Mark.

"Oh my!" exclaimed Ellie as she turned the object over to reveal the face on the reverse. She seemed to lose her train of thought but quickly regained it. "There is one person I know, Jim Anderson. He's a member of our historical society. He is actually a history professor and he also has a fair knowledge of the occult too. If anyone can translate it he's your man or he'd know someone who could. Do you want me to give him a ring?"

"That would be great mum. Now I know roughly how old it is I'm even more interested. I thought maybe three hundred years old but sixteen hundred is surprising."

"Back in a mo," Ellie said as she moved towards the corner of the room where the cordless handset was sitting in it's holder and she sat in the chair next to the table it was on.

Jack took the amulet from Mark and began to examine it. He turned it over and over in his long fingers and finally said. "Be careful, by the look of that chap on the back I doubt it was used for any good all those years ago. You know I'm not superstitious but that thing gives me bloody chills."

"I know what you mean dad. I don't get a great vibe from it but I'm just interested in where it came from and how it got buried in the roots of a tree in a field miles from anywhere."

Ellie put the phone back in it's dock and walked over. "Jim is intrigued, can you see him this evening if you have nothing planned?"

"As long as we're not putting him out, that's fine. We were only going to chill out before getting back to the grind tomorrow."

"He said he was marking essays and could do with a break. Here's his address." Ellie handed over a post-it with a Paddenham location and phone number.

"Thanks mum, seeing him today and maybe getting some answers is a lot better than wondering about the thing all week.

They spent the next couple of hours playing Scrabble. Girls against Boys. After their third straight defeat Jack said, "Next time I get to pair up with this young lady. I'm starting to get an inferiority complex. I need some help," he laughed.

"Thanks for the vote of confidence dad," chuckled Mark.

"It's not you, it's me, you know numbers are my game and not words. Maybe we can play Yahtzee. I'm good at that." The other three giggled at his feigned petulance.

"What about Noughts and Crosses?" goaded Ellie.

Mark decided they needed to make a move to get to see the professor over in Paddenham. It was about fifteen miles there and almost twenty back to his flat on the by-pass.

"Thanks for a lovely meal mum and thanks for setting us up with your friend."

"Happy to. Are you coming over next Sunday? I have a pork recipe I want to try out on you and it's a bit better than those bacon sandwiches you seem to live on. I've heard about that," she winked at Nat.

"Well to avoid me being nagged about my salt intake I suppose I'd better." He hugged her and then shook his dad's hand. Jack gave Nat a big hug and then Ellie gave her an even bigger one.

"Don't forget about what we talked about," Jack reminded Mark. The younger man could just about detect a blush forming on Nat's cheeks and guessed that his mum had indeed been having a similar conversation in the living room. The trip over to the history professor could be awkward he thought. First Steve and Kim were matchmaking and now his parents. It was a bloody conspiracy!

They got in the car and both waved at Jack and Ellie and Mark saw the conspiratorial smile on Jack's face to confirm his thought then he reversed down the drive and into the lane where his parents lived. He headed toward Paddenham and maybe some answers, maybe even more questions.

They arrived in Paddenham a little after four. Mark found the house on the outskirts of the town quite easily. It was a small Victorian property, the dark red brick was sparsely covered with ivy. There were bay windows upstairs and downstairs at the front and a short set of steps led up to the front door, bright red with an ornate iron knocker. Mark tapped lightly with the knocker and within thirty seconds the door opened and a rather large man with a short black and grey beard stood before them, He was in his fifties and was wearing glasses with tiny round lens perched at the end of his bulbous nose.

"Professor Anderson?" asked Mark.

"Call me Jim, I've been expecting you."

They moved through an almost too narrow hallway, Jim's shoulders brushing the walls, and into a small room at the far end on the left. Obviously it was his study. The walls were covered with bookcases full with hundreds of hard back books and judging by the thickness and age of them Mark assumed they weren't fiction. There were two wide desks in the room, both covered with stacks of paper and one had a large computer monitor with wires trailing down underneath the desk to a PC.

"Please, take a seat," Anderson said, "Forgive the chaos but I've been marking essays all weekend. Can I get you tea or coffee?"

Mark and Nat both politely declined, eager to get on with the job at hand. Mark took the rough grey amulet from his pocket and handed it to the professor.

"This is what my mum asked you about, she estimated the date at around 400-500 AD and recognised the writing as Runic. That's pretty much all we know about it."

"Your mother said you found it buried in the roots of a tree. I doubt it was dropped there and the tree had grown on that spot over the years. The grey colour would easily be picked out in the grass or mud as soon as the owner had realised it was missing. It has a rather curious heat coming from it, much more than from merely being in your pocket."

"I noticed that as soon as I picked it up, it was in the shade when I found it and thought it was strange."

"Your mother was pretty accurate with the dating of it - around 460 AD. About 50 years after the Romans left Britain to deal with their own troubles at home. There was a return to Paganism in a lot of areas when they left so seeing the Pagan symbolism is no surprise. The fellow on the reverse side is clearly some demon and would possibly be a minion of the person the amulet was designed to ward off or maybe something to call on to invoke a spell. I'll need to do a bit of research to determine that.

He stared at the figures I ᚠᛁᛚᛚ ᚱᛖᛏᚢᚱᚾ and ᛋᛁᛋ ᚠᛁᛚᛚ ᛗᛁᛗ which were engraved into the stone.

Anderson walked to the large bookcase near the window, his giant frame set against the greying net curtains. "Ah, here it is. I assume your mother told you about my interest in the occult, or rather the history of the occult in Britain to be more accurate. I'm not a Satanist or a Warlock or anything like that. I'm just interested in the historical aspect of the beliefs people had. Like a biblical scholar if you will, but at the other end of the spectrum, and witches are my speciality. Even today there are still many covens in this county. A friend once joked that there were more active covens in Hertfordshire than there were chip shops."

"Yes, she did mention you were pretty much an authority on the subject," replied Mark.

"How kind," he said with a slight half smile as he leafed through the book in his hands. "Right, in the mid-fifth century in Hertfordshire there were many witches. It was not illegal in those days and they weren't hunted down like during the roughly 100 years between Queen Elizabeth's reign and the famous persecutions enacted by men like Matthew Hopkins in the mid-seventeenth century. Most witches from the period this stone was made were so-called white witches who were basically your healers and herbalists and the same is true today."

"With you so far," said Mark, even more interested than before. "I'm guessing this thing has nothing to do with a white witch then?"

"It may have been passed down to a white witch but there were a few powerful witches who practised the dark arts. These were no characters from fairy tales, they existed, and their magic apparently worked. Curses were the main thing. If you had an enemy or someone else you wanted to see dead so you could steal their land you'd go and see one of these dark witches and paid them to curse your nemesis. As I said, these spells apparently worked. Maybe it was auto-suggestion and the person cursed found out and their belief was so strong they literally talked themselves into dying or someone died from an accident and that was put down to the curse, who knows? But it's evident that people did die one way or another after being targeted by the witch. But the majority of these people just kept to their healing rituals and potions though."

"Any idea who it belonged to?"

"Maybe the best known witch or healer in this area in the fifth century was a woman called Kendra Watkin, she was from a long line of occultists both dark and light. Her grandmother was supposed to be very powerful. It was rumoured the grandmother could even resurrect the dead. Kendra comes from the Old English and means *knowing*."

"So what happened to her?"

"No one knows for sure, she just vanished apparently. Obviously there are very little in the way of records from that time, just stories passed down from generation to generation. It seems to be a complete mystery at the moment.

"You've answered a lot of questions and also posed others I'd never even thought of. Thank you for your help and I hope to hear from you soon, hopefully with the mystery solved."

"Solving this could benefit me too, there may be a book in this. It would get me away from grading essays for a while," laughed Anderson. "Can I hold onto the amulet for a while? I'd like to take a few snaps and send them to a friend who may be able to help us out."

"Yes, of course," Mark said as he handed over the stone, feeling the strange heat emanating from it.

Both visitors shook Jim's hand and walked to the car. Nat was strangely silent as she had been throughout the entire encounter with the large professor.
Steve was tackling the long back garden and looking forward to putting his feet up with a nice cold lager. He trimmed the privet hedges first as that was the biggest job. His back garden was twice the size of the front and the hedges separated him from his neighbours on either side. He quite liked the neighbours on both sides but still wanted a bit of privacy. Especially in the summer when both he and Kim like to sunbathe on the back lawn, trying to get a tan started before they went on their summer holidays to somewhere hot. Last year it was Tunisia which was great. The Bardo Museum and the Carthage National Museum were the particular highlights of that two week break. It was just the two of them with their two boys, Justin and John, staying at their grandparents and causing mayhem as usual.

With the privet screen of the garden nicely trimmed he went in for a glass of water and then putting the portable electric clippers away pulled out the hover mover. He plugged the mower's power lead into the inside socket of the shed in the corner of the garden and started to mow the lawn up and down at right angles to the house almost tasting the ice cold beer that was waiting for him in the fridge. The grass was fairly long and it was slow going to cut the green carpet of his back garden. He was thinking his old mower would have clogged up by now with the long grass wrapped around the spindle that held the rotating blades. He was happy he'd upgraded this year to something a bit better that could handle the first cutting of the season without a problem. He decided to stop at the halfway point for a smoke. He fished the half full packet and lighter out of the thigh pocket of his camouflage trousers and lit up, the smoke drawn deep into his lungs. He'd have to give up, he thought, aware that he was getting to the age where a heart attack or stroke was a possibility as well as the obvious threat of various cancers. He owed it to his kids more than anything. It would certainly cost him less money with the price of a packet approaching thirteen quid and with a government budget coming up in the next week smokers will be hit again as well as motorists and drinkers so it was a triple-whammy for someone like him. He felt he was earning less and less every year and was grateful that Kim was working full time in the hairdressers now. It would be hard to make ends meet without her money, especially at Christmas when the kids demanded the latest gadgets. Yes, he'd try to give up the smokes again, after next weekend, one final week and then start saving sixty or seventy quid a week. Put that money in a savings account and watch it add up plus earn what they laughingly call interest now. Steve liked to plan for the future.

His garden backed onto the farmer's fields and he stood and took in the view as he smoked. Sheep were grazing, all of them marked with a red splotch of dye that identified them as Charlie's flock. At the end of that long field was a line of trees that hid a track which led downhill to the farm. That track had several turn-offs that gave access to every field on the large property. Steve could see just beyond the trees that a line of mist was slowly rolling in. He thought it was pretty unusual in the afternoon in this area but shrugged it off as part of the weird weather that was becoming more and more common in recent years. He could see a dark shape standing very still in the mist. If he had paranoid tendencies he could imagine the person watching him but he thought it was just a walker stopping to rest, take a drink or adjust an item of clothing. They were certainly taking their sweet time over it. Maybe they were making a call on their mobile. The signal round here was pretty decent for a rural area and maybe they wanted to have a conversation without panting their way up the slight incline towards the newly planted corn. Every year Steve had planned to go over there and take a few ears of corn for a barbecue but when he was ready the corn had always disappeared, harvested almost overnight.

He finished his smoke and flicked the butt into the field and walked back to the orange mower. He checked the power lead was nowhere near the base and pulled the short trigger on the handle. Nothing. He pulled at the small plastic starter a couple of more times with no response. Then he walked to the shed and through the door to see if the cut-out had tripped for some reason but it was still in the on position so there should be power going to the mower. Maybe the blades were clogged with the long grass? He pulled the plug out of the socket in the shed and took a small set of hand shears from the nail in the wall they were hanging on. He trudged back to the new grass cutter he now thought of as the 'useless piece of shit' and turned it on it's side. There was nothing around the blades. He then gave them a spin and they rotated easily. Definitely nothing restricting them he thought. It must be an electrical fault. He'd need to take it back to the garden centre he'd bought it from after work tomorrow. Obviously annoyed he tried to think on the bright side and he'd get his ice cold lager a little bit earlier than anticipated. Just as he was about to turn the machine back over and carry it to the shed to be boxed up he could feel a slight vibration on the plastic casing. The blades then started to spin, slowly at first then picking up speed. But there was no power! The plug was removed, he was sure! He looked at the whirling cutting tool and became a little fuzzy headed. He tried to let go of the warm casing but found he couldn't. It was like his hands were impossibly magnetised to the plastic, he just couldn't release it. He was feeling dizzy now, mesmerised by the revolving razor sharp blades. His face moving lower and lower towards them.

Kim was doing the ironing when she heard an agonising scream from the garden. She ran through the ground floor to the sliding door that separated the dining room from the patio. She could see Steve slumped over the upturned mower, it was no longer orange but a dark crimson. There was also a thick spray of blood in a three foot semi circle where Steve's head should have been. She knew it was hopeless, there was nothing she could do. She sat in shock, unable to move, knowing that nothing would ever be the same again, she was numb. Surely she should be wailing and in tears? She found guilt in herself that she was unable to. Maybe they would come later? Much later. Eventually she dialled for an ambulance.
The boys came home from an afternoon at their friend's house but were immediately sent back there, she didn't want them glimpsing the scene in the back garden. Their lives had already changed in a split second and she didn't want them traumatised too.

The Jag pulled up in front of Mark's flat at a little past seven. During the drive Mark had had a blinding pain behind his left eye. Luckily the road wasn't too busy and he safely steered the car over to the side and sat for a moment, the pain now gone.

"What's wrong babe?" asked Nat.

"I just had pain in my eye for a second, like a flash of light, seems fine now," he said.

"Must have been my dazzling beauty," she joked. "Are you sure you're okay?"

"Good now, just one of those things I suppose … or your dazzling beauty," he smiled.

He could see a police car parked near Steve's house and wondered what was going on. He wasn't going to bother anyone tonight and would be nosey and give Steve a ring tomorrow from work. Maybe one of the neighbours had been up to something.

They weren't too hungry so decided to watch a film and snack during it. He still had a couple of bags of microwave popcorn left from their last film night. They both loved horror films but Mark thought the main reason Nat liked them was so she could snuggle up to Mark and feel protected. He didn't mind as long as marriage didn't crop up. Why was he so averse to the idea? His parents were a great example of a relationship that worked and he loved kids too. And he did want to be a dad, desperately.

He really didn't fancy anything too cerebral so settled for the original *Night of the Living Dead.* He liked Romero because you didn't have to think too much with his films and they were easy to relax to if you didn't take the gore too seriously. He set the DVD up while Nat got the popcorn microwaved. The DVD had both the black and white version and a colourised copy too but he went for the more atmospheric original black and white. Nat came back to the front room with a big bowl of popcorn drizzled with honey and a roll of kitchen towels under her arm. She sat next to him and Mark started the DVD. They watched the old car drive to the cemetery and a few minutes later the brother uttered the immortal words 'They're coming to get you Barbara!' and things went pretty much downhill for the heroine from that point.

Monday April 20th

Mark woke at seven that morning. Nat had stayed the night and was still asleep next to him. She didn't need to get to work until noon as she was just doing a half-day but Mark had to be at work at nine. He made his way to the bathroom and had a quick shower and shave, applied the after shave balm that Nat had bought him for his birthday and moved into the kitchen and had a light breakfast clad only in a fluffy white bath towel. He finished his second cup of coffee and then crept into the bedroom and dressed quickly in his dark grey suit that he hated. In fact, he hated all his suits but the company insisted they all dress professionally even if the potential customers couldn't see him at the other end of the phone. Apparently if you look good you feel good and the customer will pick that up. The majority of the people he spoke to were too thick to pick their noses without written instructions he thought.

At around eight he left the flat for the drive to the office. At this time of day it usually took forty-five minutes for the four mile trip. He was usually stressed by the delays and congestion by the time he got there, but his music got him through. He bought a black coffee from the mobile kiosk that sat in the large car park. The building housed several other companies who did virtually the same as his. Cold calling customers with various third rate products, convincing them that the services were better than they already had and when the customer realised they weren't they found they were stuck in a contract and needed to pay a hefty release fee or stick with it until the long contract ended.
He hated conning people like that but it seemed he was stuck in this job for now. It was salary plus a good commission so he just couldn't leave until he found something with the same income and good jobs like that where morals were applied were pretty rare. He was in a rut and he knew it. Maybe that was another reason he wasn't keen on marriage at the moment. He thought if the pressure was on him to provide for Nat and possibly a couple of kids he'd never have the nerve to make a change. He took the lift to the shabby third floor and walked past a few identical offices housing identical dodgy companies like the one he worked for.

"Morning, you old tosser," greeted Mark from the cubicle next to his. It was the usual banter from Paul Lomax, an eighteen year old kid who thought he was God's gift, and he was getting pretty tired of it now. Lomax was tall and dark haired, wearing a light grey suit his mum must have chosen for him. His designer stubble failed to mask the acne on his thin face.

"Morning," said Mark with zero enthusiasm and set his coffee down and booted up the work PC in front of him.

"All here?" said the office manager John Laughton who virtually bounced out of his office like Tigger. Mark though he was overly effeminate and always trying to 'perform'. "I've got the figures back from base just now and we had a decent week but they want better. I know you can do it, so let's put on a big smile for the people on the other end of the phone. If they hear you are confident in the product it will breed confidence in them."

Usual corporate bullshit, thought Mark as he put on his headphones and dialled the first number on his list.

By the end of the afternoon Mark had successfully conned enough people to have hit his target for the day and make fair inroads into Tuesday's. He didn't want to hang around in that dump any longer than he had to. He wanted to pick Nat up from work and go for a drink. He really needed one.

In the car he remembered to ring Steve and got the message that Steve's work phone was turned off. That was unusual for him as he was always taking calls for his job as a mobile mechanic. If he couldn't answer at the time you could always leave a message for him and he never failed to get back to the caller.

He started the car and used the CD changer to select a different disc. Classic Whitesnake boomed out of the speakers, he preferred the Bluesy era of the band more than the later US hair rock inspired stuff. He sang along to *Walking in the Shadow of the Blues* as he drove through the business sector of the town. He wasn't a great singer but in the car or on his walks it really relaxed him and in his head he sounded better than David Coverdale.

Luckily there was a free space in front of the jewellers where Nat worked. He was there around ten minutes before she finished for the day so he tried Steve's phone again with the same result. So strange.

Back at the office Paul Lomax had been filling out and filing his paperwork, the office manager had gone not long after Mark and had left Paul to lock up when he was finished with his admin. He was just about to leave when he looked out of the window and saw there was a thick blanket of fog enveloping the car park. He couldn't even see his boy racer red Corsa which he thought was so cool but not realising he was ridiculed for spending a fortune on tinted windows, mag wheels and body panels to make the car seem wider and worst of all a bloody big spoiler on the back. Too stupid to realise that he could have spent all that money on a ten year old BMW or Merc.

He thought he saw something dark in the hazy gloom, thinking it was another worker making their way to their own car. The shape was stationary though, maybe the fog was so thick they were trying to get their bearings or had simply forgotten where they had parked that morning. He thought he heard faint words come from the fog but thought that impossible as the offices were double-glazed. He hadn't seen fog this thick for years and wasn't looking forward to trying to find his own car.

Paul got a funny feeling there was something he had to do. As if in a trance he walked to the printer and removed the black power cord from the machine and the wall socket and moved to the main office door. On the way he held onto a chair and absently dragged it behind him. He placed the padded chair next to the door and stood on it. He then knotted the power lead around the clothes hook on the back of the door and the remainder he wrapped around his thin neck and then paused for a few seconds. He then managed to kick the chair away from under him and his body weight tightened the plastic cord around his neck. He suddenly snapped out of his trance and realised what was happening. What was he doing? Why? He grappled with the lead suspending him from the hook on the door but it was just too tight and getting tighter. He couldn't breathe and his head felt like it was full of cotton wool as his oxygen was slowly running out. Flashbacks from his relatively short life came to him. His first bicycle, red with stabilisers and a honky horn, birthday parties with his friends from nursery school, holidays with his parents, the day he bought his car. Paul started to panic knowing that there would be no more memories if he couldn't free himself. He kicked his short legs backwards against the door, hoping someone from another office would hear and investigate what the noise was but no one came. No one would be there until the next morning. His struggles became less and less frequent as his strength deserted him. He slipped into a state of peace and acceptance in the end.
In the fog the tall figure laughed and disappeared into the gloom.
Mark waited outside the jewellers shop and got another severe stabbing pain in his left eye. It only lasted a second again and he dismissed it, like the first, as just 'one of those things'.

Nat exited the shop as the owner locked the door and glanced over at Mark in the Jag. He was jealous of the fact that a nobody like Mark could attract a girl like Nat and she wasn't interested in a successful businessman like himself, maybe one day he'd show her what she was missing.

Nat jumped into the passenger side of the car and kissed Mark then looked at her boss and saw the silent rage on his red face. She knew he fancied her but had never told Mark about the constant lewd looks and innuendo that came from her employer. In another few months she would hopefully be qualified as a psychotherapist, or at least training to be one and she could say goodbye to this idiot. On the other hand she could buy her engagement ring from his shop. She giggled to herself at the thought.

"What's so funny?" asked Mark.

"Nothing much, just thinking I'll be out of that place soon."

"Yes, you'll be Hertfordshire's own Freud and your own boss."

"Hopefully Sigmund and not Clement, theres a long way to go. I'll be doing NHS work for at least three years to get experience before I could ever join a private practice."

"Finger's crossed Pixie," he smiled.

"And then I'll be able to work out why you call me that!" she said and they both laughed.

Mark drove to The Lamb, a country pub a couple of miles away in a very small village they both liked. He couldn't stand the pubs in town, full of loud youngsters who were probably jobless and stank of cannabis and chip shop oil. Nat sat in a booth close to the smoldering fire waiting to be re-fuelled with logs before the bar got busy again. She liked it like this, it wasn't too hot. Mark stood at the bar and ordered a pint of Stella for himself and a gin and tonic for Nat. He exchanged a few pleasantries with the Polish barman and nodded to the old boy wearing a flat cap who was usually perched at the end of the bar who growled a greeting and went back to his pint. He sat next to Nat and sipped his lager already beginning to unwind.

"How did you do today, babe?" she asked.

"Well the day started off with the manager telling us we should all up our game then minced off into his office and I never saw him again all day. Then I spent all day on the phone ripping off everyone and hit my target easily. I hate it!"

"Didn't you have lunch?"

"Just a cup of coffee from the kiosk in the car park," he said.

"Then we'll eat here, my treat."

Twenty minutes later they were on their second round of drinks when their food arrived. Steak and ale pie with mash and peas for Mark while Nat settled for a chicken salad followed by a lovely strawberry cheesecake which they shared, although Nat ate the majority of it.

"Feel better now?" asked Nat after their plates were clean.

"That was delicious, not up to my mum's standard of course but it did fill me up." He rubbed his stomach in exaggerated satisfaction.

They got up and waved goodnight to the barman and drove back to Mark's place. Mark wanted to go for a quick walk to work off all those calories before he started to relax and Nat decided to go with him. She needed to get into her coursework after the weekend but at the same time she wanted to spend more time with Mark. The work can wait until tomorrow, she'd drink plenty of coffee and struggle on until midnight. Maybe the day after too.

They both changed into something comfortable and then walked up the hill to the fields. No lights were on at Steve and Kim's house. Mark mentioned to her about trying to call Steve a couple of times and the phone was off.

"Maybe something happened to Kim's mum in Nottingham. She hasn't been too great recently," said Nat.

"Yeah, that's probably it. They would drop everything to drive up there on short notice. Steve can't have had much time to set up a new voice mail before they went."

"I hope she's okay."

Enjoying the calm evening they moved onto the path to the fields and instead of turning right towards the short bridge over the by-pass as Mark had done on Saturday they turned left on the track which would take them through the farm and then back along the main road before turning left again to get back home. On the way down Nat looked over to Steve's house in the distance across the field, totally unaware of the tragedy of the day before.

They reached the bottom of the slight incline and on their left they saw a couple of white goats roaming pretty free in a large pen and beyond them a small chicken run with a coop. To the right was a huge barn that was still a quarter full with rolls of winter feed. Hay covered with plastic stacked almost to the roof. Next to that were the milking sheds. Charlie sold most of his milk to supermarkets but some was sold as 'raw milk' in the farm shop. It is milk that has not been pasteurised which meant it hadn't gone through the heating process that apparently makes it safer to drink although the people who buy it say it tastes better and benefits their immune system. Mark had used it a few times and really liked the taste and the thicker texture, much creamier than his usual semi-skimmed.

They exited the farm onto the path along the main road and fifteen minutes later they were back at the flat after a short uphill journey and were relaxing again. Nat was watching some reality rubbish on the TV and Mark was on his old laptop trying to find out more about this Kendra woman without much success. He hoped Professor Jim had more luck. There was plenty of information about witches but not much from the time of the amulet. The period wasn't called the Dark Ages for nothing.

During the night Ellie woke with the feeling of being choked, gasping, trying to get some air into her lungs, dull pain behind her eyes. She lay in bed and gently massaged her throat which felt like it was burning and bruised. She quietly got out of bed, trying not to disturb Jack, and went to the en suite bathroom and gulped a glass of cool water which helped sooth her throat. She got back into bed again and lay on her back thinking what could have caused her breathless panic. Was it a dream? She eventually drifted off back to sleep.

Tuesday April 21st

Mark arrived an hour late for work the following day and as soon as he entered the office he sensed something was wrong. There were a couple of men in cheap suits he didn't recognise and the manager John had red eyes as though he had been crying.

"Mark Mason?" enquired the older of the two strangers as John moved back to his office and closed the door silently.

"Yes, what's going on, was there a break-in?"

"No, Mr. Mason, take a seat." Mark sat at the nearest desk obediently. "My name is Detective Inspector Gerry Daly and this is Sergeant James Weatherby. We're here because your colleague Paul Lomax appears to have taken his own life after everyone left the office last evening."

"What, why… shit!" He didn't like Paul much but it was still a shock.

"Were you aware of any personal problems he may have had?" asked the Inspector.

"No, to be honest I didn't know much about him outside the office. I know he put a lot of money into that car of his but he made good commission here so I don't think he could have been in debt over that. As for relationship worries I have no idea, he never talked of a girlfriend, or a boyfriend for that matter."

"That pretty much confirms what your manager told us. His parents too. All he cared about was his car and the parents said he wasn't in debt and was a happy lad generally. Usually there is an obvious motive and a note as well but there's nothing, either here or at home."

"Do you mind if I ask how he did it?"

"Your manager, Mr. Laughton, had trouble opening the main office door when he arrived this morning and found him hanging on the other side and a chair overturned on the floor. Our lads removed the body about fifteen minutes before you arrived. Incidentally, you are late for work this morning, any particular reason?"

"I had to drop my girlfriend at work and there was an accident blocking the road so we were both late. I had to make a detour. I tried to ring but there was no answer."

"Where was the accident?" asked the Sergeant.

"Ratcliffe Road, you're making me feel like a suspect."

"Just routine questions, sir," answered the Inspector. "There's no doubt in my mind that it was suicide and your lateness was just a coincidence."

"Sorry, it's just the shock making me a bit sensitive."

"Quite understandable. Anyway your manager said you could take the day off as soon as I'd finished with you. If I need to get in touch I have your home and mobile numbers … that's routine too," he smiled.

Mark left the office still in a state of disbelief. He just couldn't figure out why Paul had taken his own life. He realised he didn't know him that well and he thought he was a bit of a fool but it was still unexpected. He walked to his old Jaguar and got in and just sat there for a while, contemplating how he could even motivate himself to be at work tomorrow. He decided to go for a drive to clear his head, blast some tunes out of the stereo and maybe have a pint somewhere before he called Nat to tell her the news. He headed out of the car park while hitting number six on the CD changer, his favourite compilation disc that was never removed from the changer when he rotated the discs from the leather CD cases he kept in the car boot. All his favourites were there and first on the disc was *Wishing Well* by Free. Paul Rodgers wrapped his voice around a classic tune covered by quite a few bands including Gary Moore. Mark sang along loudly as he headed to the country and a bit of peace and solitude.

After a while he drove through Marsham while listening to The Sweet's *Ballroom Blitz*, probably more well known now as being sung by that gorgeous girl in Wayne's World. The small rural village was looking peaceful and almost deserted. He'd love to live in this part of the county but the house prices were well out of his range, even renting was over a grand a month. He did see one old woman coming out of the newsagents and disappear into the butchers. He thought of the fine selection of meat usually available there and realised just how hungry he was. It was still about an hour before The Peacock in the high street opened and he could have lunch. To pass the time he drove towards the outer edge of the village and the Marsham Stones. He arrived a few minutes later and parked in the area everyone used as an ad-hoc car park, just a small patch of grass people used when they visited the neolithic site or, more likely, took their dogs for a stroll. He knew of a professional dog walker who brought five or six animals up there in her van. He knew he didn't fancy trying to control several excited dogs at the same time as well as clearing up after them but supposed the walker could see the benefit or maybe it was just the money they cared about.

He ambled through the copse towards the site relieved that there had been no rain as he was in his work clothes, mud on his shoes wouldn't do his mood or the carpets in his Jag much good. He'd bought the used, dark blue 2001 X Type from a dealer about three years previously. It had quite low mileage even now and was by far the best car he'd ever had, much better than the Kia he'd driven before the Jag. It was a three litre automatic and just cruised beautifully whether on a motorway or a country lane. He intended to get a newer Jaguar in future as he was now a huge fan of the make. His dad had offered to fund him but as usual Mark's independent streak stopped him from taking up the offer. Maybe one day soon, he just needed to save for a bit longer.

He arrived at the stone circle and he meandered around lost in thought. It really was so relaxing there despite the slight energy he picked up by each stone in turn as he slowly passed them. They were estimated to have been erected around five thousand years before, eleven of them in all, and amazingly none had fallen over and hauled up again to it's full height like many had at Avebury. He'd been to Avebury several times as well as West Kennet Long Barrow and Silbury Hill when on trips down through Wiltshire to Bristol or the West Country. The last trip was with

Nat a few months ago when they had visited Tintagel Castle, reputedly the site of King Arthur's Camelot. It was November and very windy and the steps up to the top were so steep even he and Nat struggled but once up there it was worth it for the view and the experience of quite possibly standing in the footprints of England's greatest king. The sea flung itself against the rocks used as defence against an attack by boat and Mark didn't think it would be much calmer even in summer.

There were other stone circles that Mark wanted to visit but most were a lot farther North like the Rollright stones in the Cotswolds and Castlerigg in the Lake District and he'd seen great pictures of some in the remote Scottish islands too. Maybe one day he'd visit them all, Nat would love to go too. She felt the power of the granite slabs as much as he did and they did like to get away for the odd weekend as much as they could, cash and weather permitting.

Mark wondered about the ceremonies performed there and the other sites. Were they just burials and celebrations of summer and winter solstice, or were they used for other things. The professor talked of the Pagans from around the time that the amulet was made. Were the stones used for witchcraft practices too? Had Kendra Watkin stood at this very spot reciting curses and incantations? He thought it was very possible. He knew she was from this area. He tried to imagine what she looked like. Was she was beautiful or an ugly old hag, dark hair, white and straggly or flame red? What type of clothes did she wear? Some sort of hessian sackcloth or flowing robes of silk or cotton? Hopefully Jim could answer a lot of his questions. The witches of the later period in the sixteenth and seventeenth centuries were fairly well known and well documented. There were countless accounts from the clergy of the time as well as the chroniclers and biographers of the rabid witch hunters like Matthew Hopkins, John Stearne and Roger Nowell but very little was known in comparison of the earlier witches of the fifth century and later. He thought Jim would have a lot more resources than merely the Google search he'd tried the previous evening.

An hour later he was sitting in the pub deep in thought nursing a cheese and ham ploughman's lunch and a pint of lager when his phone rang. It was Nat.

"Hi Pixie, I was just about to call you."

She was sobbing. "Steve's dead, babe."

"What? How did it happen?" He felt ice cold as shock hit him. He couldn't think, couldn't react. Steve was his best friend.

"It was an accident in his garden on Sunday afternoon, he somehow fell on the lawn mower while it was running. Kim and the boys are at her mum's which is why you couldn't get hold of anyone."

"Jesus, that's just terrible, he was such a good mate, it's not like him to do something stupid like that. Bloody hell! I have some similar news. You know that guy at work who I thought was a real dickhead, Paul Lomax? The manager found him hanging in the office this morning, it's a complete mystery why he did it. No apparent problems in his life according to his parents."

"Oh my God! I think I met him at your Christmas party, he didn't seem so bad. A bit shy maybe."

"He was just a bit cocky at work. Not really the insular type who would hang themself though in my opinion. There must have been something that made him do it," said Mark.

"Who knows what other people think about? It's a shame some people can't talk to others about their problems. They bottle it all up and then snap and no one can tell why unless they leave a note or something. Did he?"

"No, nothing in the office or at home apparently, the police told me that earlier. Just another suicide to them at the end of the day. I doubt they'll use up resources trying to find a reason. Case closed, I suppose."

"I know I was going to catch up with coursework tonight but I really don't want to be alone, do you mind?"

"Of course not. I'll pick you up from work at your usual time, I have the rest of the day off so I'll get down to the gym and try and zone out for a bit. I'm in the pub at Marsham at the moment. Just went for a drive and ended up at the stones and decided on lunch here."

"You take care and don't drink too much, Mark."

"I fancy getting rat-arsed but you know two is my limit if I'm driving. I'll grab a bottle each for us from the supermarket later and we'll toast Steve tonight. I'll probably take tomorrow off anyway. I may need to after the booze I intend on downing tonight. Shit, what a day!"

"Sounds like a plan, I couldn't concentrate on college stuff tonight anyway. I'll see you at five-thirty then?"

"I'll be there. Love you Pixie."

"Love you back babe, bye."

Mark picked at his ploughman's for the next half hour and thought about Steve. He was his best mate even though he was a bit older than Mark. One of those guys you instantly get on with. They'd had some good times over the years, watching football, going fishing in the local canal and trout lake and the odd gig too. They liked the same music, Steve was a big Blues fan and even had recordings of Robert Johnson in his prized vinyl collection. He wondered when the funeral was and was sure Kim needed help with the arrangements. There would be so much to do and he and Nat would help as much as was needed. He abandoned the remains of his lunch and left to drive home to change for the gym.

Mark really couldn't get into his exercise session but kept going as much as he could. After a little run on the static bike he ended up on the treadmill and just walked and walked at the same pace as if in a trance for more than an hour, well over three miles. He'd also brought his swimming shorts with him and decided to cool off in the pool for a while. It wasn't too busy. Two swimmers were doing lengths in a roped off area of the pool and a couple of old ladies bobbed around and chatted in their fluorescent one piece suits, one pink and the other lime green. One of them had a white swimming cap with chunky pink and yellow flowers stuck on. Mark remembered a boy at school who had forgotten his thin rubber cap for their swimming lesson and the sadistic sports master had made him wear a flowery one. Mark thought that would probably be classed as child abuse now and a baying mob of angry parents would have strung him up from the nearest basketball hoop. Mark bobbed himself for a while and then repeatedly got out of the pool and dived back in, well away from the two old dears.

After the gym and pool he found a quiet spot and just sat and listened to music in the car. Thunder, Foreigner, Queen and Black Star Riders had kept him company while he thought. Currently it was Gillan's *No Laughing In Heaven* and he chuckled at the prospect of Steve having the neighbours up in the clouds in stitches with his constant jokes. There definitely would be a few laughs. He'd undeniably miss Steve. He just wanted some time alone. Just what the hell was Steve doing messing around with a lawn mower, or anything mechanical, while it was still powered? He knew better than that, he was an experienced mechanic and wouldn't make a basic error like that. It would be second nature to safely deal with anything he was working on. It was just as mysterious as the death of Paul in the office. Mark decided to ring the office and spoke to John. He told him about Steve and said he was just too messed up to be in the next day. John had told him to take the rest of the week if he needed to as he would be taking a few days off himself and was only there to finish the reams of paperwork he had to fill out for head office as Paul had died on company premises. Mark said he'd let John know when he'd be back. He probably needed a few days.

Mark picked Nat up after she'd finished work and took her back to the flat and they hugged and talked. Nat had liked Steve and treated him like a big brother. She told Mark that she'd got a call on her mobile from Kim that morning who told her about the accident and they both sobbed for several minutes. Kim was understandably devastated. Steve and her had been together since they were both sixteen and had built their whole lives around each other and the kids and it had all been taken away in one Sunday afternoon. Luckily the boys were off playing football in the local park with their friends when it happened and were shuffled off to their friends house again. They were luckily spared the sight of their father's remains slumped over the garden machinery. Nat said that Kim and the two boys would stay with her mum in Nottingham until Saturday morning and then travel back to make arrangements for the funeral and she asked if Mark and Nat could take time off to help her and Nat had agreed without a moments hesitation for the pair of them. Mark said he would have done the same. Kim needed them, all her family were around the Nottingham area and she didn't really have anyone close down here apart from Mark and Nat. She was a bit shy.

They decided that neither of them felt like cooking and ordered from the local Indian instead. Several spicy meat dishes with rice, naans and poppadoms were ordered by phone. They found a comedy to watch to try and lighten things, an old Adam Sandler film that didn't really seem as funny as it used to be. Maybe it was the circumstances. An hour into the film the delivery arrived and they watched the rest while munching on their curries. Mark had bought a decent bottle of scotch for himself and a litre bottle of white wine for Nat before he picked her up from work and after they had finished the Indian and put the plates in the sink and ran water over them they started on their respective drinks. Mark usually had a mixer like ginger ale or tonic water with his but tonight he drank it straight. It would have the desired effect a lot quicker. They sat on the floor propped up side by side against the sofa and talked for what seemed like hours.

Eventually, around midnight, they managed to crawl into bed and held each other until they both drifted off to sleep.

Wednesday April 22nd

Mark was shaken awake forcefully by Nat a few hours later. He felt muzzy and dehydrated from his drinking binge.

"I think someone is in the flat," she whispered.

"What? Stay here." Mark slid out of bed. He was only wearing a pair of boxer shorts and immediately felt a chill that snapped him into wakefulness. He looked around for some sort of weapon just in case Nat was right and it wasn't part of her dream. He picked up a block of glass with a large scorpion inside - a memento he had purchased from a butterfly sanctuary on a trip to the US a couple of years ago. He slowly made his way to the bedroom door. He hadn't heard anything and was hoping it was just Nat's imagination working overtime. He stood at the door and listened intently. Still nothing. The door was open a crack and he pulled it open another inch and could see the hallway bathed in a pre-dawn half light. He thought it must have been around four-thirty or five. He opened the door a little more and slipped into the narrow hallway. The bathroom door to his right was open and he peeked in and saw nothing out of the usual. He was still reluctant to turn a light on just in case there was someone there. He didn't want any intruder to panic even though he was pretty close to it himself. He found it hard to breathe from the tension and wondered if the glass scorpion ornament would be enough to fend off anyone if he had to. The kitchen was on his left and he padded through it's door and shuddered as his bare feet hit the freezing wooden laminate flooring. He then pulled the largest knife from a block holding it with a collection of others. He didn't know if he could actually use it but maybe a deterrent was all he needed. He did notice that two of the kitchen drawers were open but that could have been Nat or himself last night while in their drunken state although he couldn't think of what they would have been looking for.

Mark moved back out to the hallway with just the front room to check. What he saw chilled him to the bone. More open drawers and cupboard doors, the cushions of the chairs and sofa removed and on the floor. The jacket of his suit which had been hanging near the front door had it's pockets ripped out. Someone had definitely been there. He turned on the light to make sure that they had definitely left and weren't hiding in a dark corner or behind a door or sofa. He called to Nat. He wanted her with him as he picked up the phone from the glass coffee table and that was when he saw the note.

GIVE IT BACK

Nat arrived from the bedroom wearing Mark's red towelling bathrobe. She saw the mess the front room was in and gasped.

"I'm sure that wasn't us, however drunk we were," she said quietly in a throaty tone needing lubrication.

"It wasn't," said Mark already dialling for the police. He showed her the note.

"What does it mean? Who was here and what do they want?"

"I have no idea, maybe they had the wrong flat?"

Mark was connected to the emergency operator and told them that someone had broken into his flat while they were sleeping. He said that the intruder had gone and had appeared to be searching for something. The operator was satisfied there was no danger that would have necessitated a patrol car being dispatched immediately and told him someone from the local station would be around as soon as possible but it may take a few hours. Mark thanked them and hung up after confirming his address and phone number. He was relieved the home invader was gone and then thought of what might have happened. Were they actually in the bedroom and watched them sleep? He rushed back and checked if anything had been disturbed. Nothing was out of place apart from the clothes that littered the floor.
He suddenly became very cold and at first he thought it may be the lack of clothes but then realised it was the much deeper chill of shock as he raised the thought they could have been murdered in their sleep. He sat on the bed and started to shake. He could do with another drink but thought a strong coffee would be better while they waited for the police to show up.

Mark and Nat were forcing themselves to eat some toast with black coffee even though they were not hungry when the doorbell rang. Nat thought she may never get her appetite back again as Mark went to answer the door. Standing in front of him was Detective Inspector Daly and his sergeant, Weatherby.

"Morning Mr. Mason. Normally we'd send a couple of plods to check on things and get a statement after a non-violent burglary but I saw your name on the incident report and thought I'd come personally."

"Come in Inspector, what makes me so special?"

"I was intrigued. Burglars don't normally leave notes."

Daly and the sergeant looked around the front room. Mark had seen enough crime shows to know that he shouldn't move anything or tidy up and the only thing he had touched was the note. He expected he'd need to have his fingerprints recorded to eliminate his from any others on the note or the furniture even though it was a near certainty that the intruder had worn gloves anyway.

"What do they want you to give back?" asked Daly.

"I haven't a clue, I haven't stolen anything in case that was your train of thought, I was hoping they'd got the wrong address."

"Possible, but I doubt it. Is there anyone with a key to your flat? I don't see any evidence of a forced entry or even signs of a pro break-in."

"The landlord has a key and the estate agent I'm renting through has a set. Also my parents have a spare. Oh, my girlfriend has her key too but she was with me last night."

"I think we can safely rule your parents and girlfriend out but I'll check the other two. I had a case a few years ago when an employee at an estate agent made copies of keys and monitored the social media of the renters to see when they went on holiday. He knew there would be no interruption when he cleaned out their property. Contact the agents and get them to send a locksmith around to change the locks."

"I will."

Nat had made tea for them all and they all moved to the kitchen to sit as the sofa's cushions were still strewn on the floor. She'd set out a plate of biscuits and a bowl of sugar. She was still visibly shaken. Daly noticed the empty scotch and wine bottles on the kitchen counter.

"So what's your name, Miss?"

"Natalie Cross, I don't mind telling you I'm scared out of my wits Inspector."

"Do you have any idea who broke in and what they were after?"

"None at all, I just can't think what anyone would want. Do you think they could be back?"

"No, I don't think so, and they wouldn't get in after the locks have been changed, we'll make checks on all the employees at the estate agent's anyway and maybe something will turn up or at least discourage a repeat performance. Obviously if we knew what they were looking for it would be helpful, a motive would narrow down the field."

The inspector rose and his sergeant followed suit a split second later. "I'll get the SOCO boys to come round and look for fingerprints, secretions and the like but I doubt they will find anything. This is the second visit to this road I've made in the last few days. Did you know the man at number twenty-nine, Steven Jones?"

"Yes, he was my best friend, we only found out yesterday when his wife called Nat. As you can see from the bottles we toasted him last night. Why would you have been called to an accident? That's not usual, is it?"

"It was the bizarre nature of the accident that interested me, lawn mower accidents are pretty standard like electrocution or running over a foot and maybe even losing a hand if someone is foolish enough to fiddle with the cutting tool but falling onto the already rotating blade was a bit strange. More gangland style in my opinion. He wasn't into anything like that, was he?"

"No, Steve was as straight as they come, just a mechanic that mostly answered call outs, mobile tuning and servicing, that sort of thing."

"Yes, that's what his boss said, thanks for confirming that. I can only put it down as a freak accident. Thanks for your help," he said as he moved towards the door. "Meanwhile try and get away for a few days, come back refreshed and the place won't seem as violated as it does now."

"That's a good idea, staying here creeps me out a bit now, I'll probably move somewhere else too," said Mark.

Four hours later the Scenes of Crimes people in their white paper suits had left and Mark and Nat decided to get out of the flat and go to the pub to discuss getting away as the inspector had suggested. They both browsed for hotels in interesting places on their phones while seated in a corner booth at the pub.

That evening they travelled to a hotel in Marlborough, Wiltshire for their break. It took less than two hours to drive down after they packed. Neither wanted to spend the night in Mark's flat after last night's frightening escapade. Neither had actually visited Stonehenge before and were keen to visit. They had a light meal of cheese sandwiches at the bar as the restaurant was closing for the night as they arrived. The bar was fairly quiet and they sat on a blue checked sofa near an open fire with an ancient brick fireplace. An hour later after a couple of drinks they retired to their room. The large double room had a low ceiling and eggshell blue walls and a beige carpet, a wide bay window took up most of one side with a view of the high street. The bathroom was huge with a clear glass shower in one corner.

Thursday April 23rd

The next morning they rose early to get a head start on the day. Breakfast in the hotel was a full English. Mark particularly enjoyed the bacon and sausages and even had an extra sausage and rasher of bacon and a slice of fried bread that Nat couldn't eat as she was so full. The coffee was excellent too, a nice Colombian brew that Mark had drunk black and Nat with milk and one of the sweeteners she always carried in her handbag.

They drove South in the early spring sunshine on the A345 towards Amesbury. It took them less than an hour to spot the signs for Stonehenge and the visitor centre. The car park was over half full already but they managed to find a spot not too far away from the massive building that finally opened in 2013 after millions in investment. They walked about 400 yards from the car to the ticket booths and paid for their passes to the centre and the neolithic site that was almost two miles away and had to be reached by a constant stream of shuttle buses. Someone tried to sell them a subscription to the National Trust but Mark politely declined saying that one trip a year to one of their sites wouldn't really be worth it.

They entered the indoor museum and were treated to many impressive exhibits including a virtual sunrise at the monoliths. There were a lot of other things like displays of stone and bone tools found at the site over the last two centuries. There was a good amount of information about how the ancient occupants of the area had lived around five thousand years ago when the stones were supposedly erected to more than three thousand years before that date. It really was remarkable thought Mark. The outside exhibition consisted of mud, wicker and thatch huts that you could enter and see the cramped conditions where the archaic tribes had lived. Although harsh conditions, Mark thought that some areas of London were not much better even now. They were packed with baskets, pottery and even primitive weapons on the walls and replicas of the fires they had to cook and heat the huts by. Nat must have taken over a hundred pictures with her digital camera. Ellie would enjoy those.

They decided to have a light lunch before getting the shuttle up to the stones even though their breakfast was less than three hours ago and still weighed heavily in Mark's stomach. They both had tomato soup and a bread roll each to keep them going until they stopped for something mid-afternoon or the evening if they could last that long.

After lunch they walked the short distance to the shuttle pick up point and only had to wait a few minutes before a green bus arrived bringing visitors back from the site. The previous passengers disembarked and then a group of about a dozen Germans pushed their way onto the bus before Mark and Nat entered and sat together. Within a couple of minutes the bus started on the short journey up to the stones. The babble from the Germans all around them was a bit annoying and Mark made a mental note to let them get a few minutes head start before he and Nat started their tour around the ring of sarsons.

It didn't take long for the bus to climb the slight incline and stop to let everyone off. It was very windy at the site and there were already about a hundred tourists there making their way on the path around the roped off area housing the stones. Nat's camera was out again although she got a bit frustrated when she lined up the perfect shot and someone drifted into the frame at the worst possible moment. Mark stood next to the rope so no one could push in front of him and allowed Nat to take her pictures resting her hands on his shoulder. One of those little things that Mark often did, thought Nat. They both looked to the skies when a flock of starlings rose in the air and did their synchronised dance, there must have been thousands of them. Nat quickly pointed her camera at them and took a few snaps, pleased that she got a few decent ones.

When they were nearing the end of their walk around the circle Mark noticed a fog rolling in from the fields on the far side of the stones. *What the hell is it with all this fog recently,* he thought to himself. It certainly was unusual for this time of year. The gloom enveloped the collection of granite and Mark thought he could see dark shapes moving between the stones. Fragments of his dream from a few nights ago fluttered in his head. He put the figures down to the people on the other side of the circle even though they seemed too near, the fog foreshortening the distance, distorting things he surmised. He felt a chill as they walked back to the bus pick up and was relieved when they were on the next vehicle on their way back to the visitor centre even if those same annoying Germans were aboard again.

That afternoon they browsed the shops of Marlborough and bought a few gifts for family and friends and generally relaxed. In the evening they dined at the hotel's restaurant. Mark devoured his beef, pancetta and red wine lasagne while Nat feasted on pan fried hake with mussel chowder. They'd only had a sandwich each while shopping and were both ravenous by the time they sat down to eat their main meal.

Not more than five minutes after Mark and Nat retired to their room and had settled down to watch some TV, Mark's mobile rang.

"Hello, Mark? It's Jim. I have a little news for you."

"That's great, what have you found out?" Mark set his phone onto speaker mode and laid it on the bed so Nat could hear the conversation.

"Well, I made a scan of the amulet and sent it to my friend in Germany. He's somewhat of an expert in Saxon and pagan rituals and between us we think we've deciphered the Runic wording around the outside."

"Brilliant. Does it make any sense?"

"I think it does, it says: 'Six will die' and 'I will return'."

"Doesn't sound too good, Any idea what it means?"

"The second part makes a lot of sense," enthused Jim. "We know Kendra Watkin was a related to a very powerful witch and necromancer. Her ultimate aim was to have eternal life. A stone, *this stone* was part of the spell or ritual for her to achieve that. The six were probably needed to achieve that, either sacrificed or by curse. I assume she was stopped somehow."

"And I uncovered it," said Mark ruefully.

"My theory, and it is only a theory, I could be completely wrong, but this was chipped off a massive obelisk like the ones at Avebury, or more likely the stones at Marsham as they are the only local ones I know of, and then it was shaped and the carvings added and would have been worn around the neck with a cord or a hide lace. It was some sort of talisman that was intended to complete her transformation into immortality. Now the big mystery as far as I'm concerned is exactly who she came up against and how did they stop her. I can't find anyone who was even on a par with her power and magic in any book I own. This person seems to have been erased from history for some reason. Her death was covered up. I know not much accurate information came out of that period but she was well known and not some anonymous peat cutter or lowly peasant. She didn't just disappear off the face of the earth.

The church was in it's relative infancy over here, maybe they had something to do with it? The local Saxon Thanes were always trying to keep on the good side of the church, something that really hasn't changed apart from the names. So another theory is she did something that offended the church and they asked the Thane to take care of it without involving the church directly. They always had a problem with magic and in their eyes there was only one true healer. And they didn't like the shine being taken off Him. All pure speculation at this point of course, as I said, I could be way off the mark."

"It would certainly be very interesting to find out. What's your next move?" asked Mark.

"I need to work out what else is on the amulet and what it means. I'm not sure yet. I have another friend I can ask, another expert on the Saxons, but he's incommunicado on a dig in Kent so I think I'll run down tomorrow and pick his brains. I also want to find out just who that chap on the back of the piece is. His identity could be very important. I just don't think he's a generic depiction of a demon. I'll call you in a couple of days."

"Okay, thanks Jim. It's all very much appreciated."

"My pleasure Mark."

Michael Cross had finished his latest shift pattern on the oil rig off the coast of Aberdeen. He worked twelve on - twelve off for three weeks and then had a two week break onshore to rest but 'rest' usually consisted of being pissed for the full two weeks. He'd been ferried back to shore by helicopter and had landed four hours previously and had gone straight to the pub. His depression meant that he bottled things up for the three week shift and then all hell let loose when he was on dry land, although 'dry' was a bit of a misnomer as it was rarely dry on the coast of Northeast Scotland. Earlier he'd had a fight with one of his crew, big Alec Forsyth, the reason forgotten. He'd gone for a walk to cool off. He was already very drunk. He drank to kill the emotional pain of his lost family. His wife and most of all his lovely daughter Natalie. He hated himself for leaving but with the wife not being able to conceive again after Natalie things just got worse for them, all the tension and regret led to accusations and spite. Ironically there had been no one else since he left twenty years ago. He could have had another life with more kids but never even tried. Guilt over leaving his family meant that he didn't want to risk doing that again to someone else. He was now fifty and and his sole aim was to save as much as he could, while he could, for his retirement although he would probably try and find something else in the area. He thought he had maybe four or five more years on the rig before his strength and will deserted him, the cold wind seemed to cut deeper into his bones as he got older despite several layers of clothing. It wasn't a game for an old man. He was born and bred in Marsham and still missed the area of his youth. There wasn't much to do but he and his friends always found something to occupy themselves with unlike kids today who have all the entertainment they need and still say they are bored. Maybe one day he could move back to be near his daughter. He hoped she, in particular, could forgive him for not being a big part of her life in the last twenty years. He used to visit several times a year and spoilt her rotten but the visits became less frequent over the years as his depression took hold of him. He hadn't even called on her birthday last year as he was in a pit of drunkenness and self-loathing. He'd even like to get on speaking terms with his ex-wife too but she truly hated him, he couldn't blame her though. It wasn't her fault that she couldn't have more kids and certainly not his - it was biology. It was way too late for them to try again, their relationship was very broken. He was lonely.

He started to cry softly as he walked, the tears barely noticeable in the fine rain beating his rugged face. He wore a set of green overalls covered with a black donkey jacket and heavy work boots. The jacket was getting heavier the more rain water that soaked into it. He really should get back to his lodgings and sleep off the booze but continued walking along the rough shingle path that ran down along the coast. Occasionally he was hit by spray from the large waves hitting the breakwater thirty feet beneath him. Most people underestimated the power of the ocean but he respected it along with everyone else who worked on or near it. The wind was getting to gale force now and he really should be turning back. Maybe have a nightcap in the pub before he went to bed. There was always time for one more. Always one more, he laughed through the tears.

Out to sea he noticed a mist forming over the waves. He thought it was strange as it was still raining but he was no meteorologist. He couldn't remember ever seeing that before but the scotch didn't do wonders for his memory at the best of times. The mist was thickening to a dense fog as it rolled towards the shore. He didn't want to get caught in that so turned and walked along the path in the direction of the town. He was near Balmedie beach so not too far to walk back to the hostel. There seemed to be such a weight on his shoulders. Twenty years of guilt weighed itself on him so much that his knees felt like buckling underneath him. Why was he feeling so melancholy all of a sudden? Much more than usual. The drink usually worked to dull his senses enough so that he could function. He felt such despair, so much more than he had ever felt, even in the first months after leaving his wife and his beautiful little girl. He checked on the progress of the fog. It was definitely nearer now and he could see a dark shape in the midst of it. Maybe an old fisherman stranded in his skiff out to catch a couple of flatfish for his supper. The turbot was great from these waters.

Michael had the urge to climb down the rocky black breakwater. He wanted to feel the full force of the gale blowing directly at him and feel the spray and the salt in the air around him. He carefully made his way down through the large rocks, he didn't want to slip. He got to the bottom and decided to sit on one of the slabs there. The water was lapping over his boots and the briny spray coated his lips but he didn't seem to mind. He stared out into the fog and then stood and walked slowly onto the bed of silt and then into the vast North Sea. Peace. The figure out to sea watched silently.

Mark sat bolt upright in the hotel bed he was sharing with Nat, the stabbing in his eye lessening. He could taste salt in his mouth this time too. Luckily he hadn't disturbed Nat and decided to keep things to himself about the pains for now. He didn't want to worry her, although he was starting to get a little worried himself. He decided if it happened again he'd go and see his doctor.

Friday April 24th

Next day of their short getaway Mark and Nat decided to visit Salisbury Cathedral, somewhere they had never been before. Although neither were in the slightest religious they loved visiting these places just for the sheer beauty of the ancient architecture. It was more a history thing with them and to witness and enjoy something that was over 800 years old filled them with excitement. They'd visited places over a thousand years old in the past. British history was something to be remembered and honoured, not tucked away like a creepy uncle at a family gathering by people offended by the past just to be trendy and politically correct.

They drove south again from Marlborough and reached Salisbury about ninety minutes later. Mark parked the Jag and found a coffee shop, ordered a couple of cappuccinos and sat outside on the terrace watching the world go by. They could see the cathedral from where they sat and it looked huge even at that distance and they looked forward to seeing it even closer. The buildings were framed by blue sky with only a few scattered wispy clouds about. The giant carved facade supported the massive spire that stands over 400 feet according to Google. The main body took thirty-eight years to complete and the whole site covered eighty acres. It really was an impressive sight to behold for the first time.

They finished their coffees and ambled slowly towards the magnificent building. As they took the long tarmac path and got closer they could make out the ornate carvings on the outside walls of the main face that housed the large arched doorway. According to the website he was using on his phone the statues were mostly from the mid-nineteenth century and were of Biblical figures. Mark recognised Moses, St. Katherine complete with her wheel, Daniel with a lion, St. George holding a dragon's head and St. Christopher carrying a small child on his shoulders. There were also figures of all the apostles both major and minor, Kings, Saints and Archbishops and also St. Alban who he knew well from St. Alban's Cathedral which was close to where he lived and where he had visited several times.

They stopped for a moment to look up at the spire. Four hundred feet may not sound a lot but up close it looked like it reached up to the sparse clouds, maybe even the heavens. Nat had her camera out and had already taken a couple of dozen pictures of the statues before pointing her lens upwards.

"That's amazing," she gushed. "So tall."

"Just wait until you get inside," said Mark. "I had a look at the virtual tour online a few weeks ago. I was hoping we'd come here on our next trip. I didn't realise it would be so soon."

They walked through the wide entrance and were immediately engulfed in a coolness that emanated from the vastness of the building. The high stone arches throughout added to the impression of being in a giant cave, they could hear people's voices carry from the distance. They trod slowly through the interior admiring the hundreds of wooden stalls, some for the choir but most for the worshippers. Mark could imagine the sound of a service echoing loud enough for their God to hear. They eventually reached the font, a vast water sculpture by William Pye which replaced the portable font that had been used for the last two hundred years. Mark had never seen anything like it before, the surface water looking as still as a black mirror while streams poured off the four corners into drains set into the stone flagged floor. Mark thought that Nat's camera battery would be running out soon she was taking so many pictures. Facebook would probably break when she uploaded them all later.

Mark asked Nat if she fancied doing the spire tour. Nat thought it was a little expensive but agreed it was one of those things you had to experience even with her extreme nervousness when it came to heights. They paid and waited in line for the tour to start.

They started to climb the short steps hugging one wall and as they ascended they had an aerial view of the nave in all it's glory, they were inches away from the gigantic stained glass windows. They went higher, above the roof of the nave, up dark wooden staircases, past a large bell and then finally found the platform on the outside of the tall tower. Nat stayed back from the parapet a few paces and handed the camera to Mark who continued to take dozens more pictures for her. The Wiltshire countryside was lovely from that height he thought. So peaceful.

After they had descended they took a trip around the cloisters and eventually found the chapter house which contained one of only four copies of the Magna Carta signed by King John in 1215. It is considered to be the best preserved of those original copies. Nat felt grateful that Britain had so much history and many parts of it were still in existence.

They were both starting to get a little hungry so decided to go and find a cafe for a late lunch. They found the perfect place on Google Maps and took the short walk west to the Salisbury Museum Cafe, part of the museum complex. They looked at the menu and agreed on a jacket potato with baked beans and grated cheese each and a traditional English cream tea to follow. Mark hadn't realised that the museum was so close to the famous cathedral. As it was barely two in the afternoon they could spend two or three hours walking around inside.

There were many excellent exhibits depicting the history of Salisbury and the surrounding area including Stonehenge but Mark was particularly interested in the early Dark Ages. The period where his find was made. The time when the Anglo-Saxons flooded the country after the Romans left and lived in a feudal society with many different tribes battling each other for decades. They brought with them a return to the paganism that was prevalent in Britain before the Romans but with a more Germanic and Nordic influence. This was Mark's favourite period of English history because there were so many questions still to be answered. The general illiteracy after the intellectuals of Rome retreated meant there was very little written history of the period, most was passed down by word of mouth and stories until the further rise of the Christian church and the recordings of daily life and more important events by the monks. The Dark Ages really did live up to it's name unlike every other period of the country's history where reams of information is available to anyone with a decent internet connection.

There were the usual collection of finds from the period like bowls, arrow and spear heads and quite a lot of brooches. There was an unusual display of masks in the shape of cats that seemed to be made from the same material as his amulet only much bigger. He found these particularly interesting. The information card said they were used in pagan rituals around 450-500 AD. He could imagine the worshippers dancing around a fire with the masks covering their faces, screaming to Woden, Balder and Hel amongst others. The pagans had many gods and many were gods of war and death and, like Balder, immortality. It was essential to revere these gods and make sacrifices to them, especially if relations with other tribes were bad at that time. Believing a god was protecting you in battle could mean the difference between life and death to the Saxons, fighting with no fear. Mark chuckled to himself when he thought that the other tribe would have the very same God on their side too.

That same afternoon Jim Anderson was on his way down to Kent to visit the dig run by his friend Stuart Pearson on the Isle of Sheppey. His big Lincoln ate up the miles on the M25 to Dartford with very little effort. It was a very big car for a very big man. He was into saving the planet and reducing his carbon footprint but couldn't really see himself in a Mini Cooper or an electric car. More like on a Mini Cooper. He moved onto the A2 which was the old Roman road of Watling Street. He'd travelled this route a few times to visit Dover Castle in the past. Getting to the top of the keep there was a bit of an effort for a man of his size but worth it once he was up there. It always amazed him that in these days of a shrinking country and a shrinking economy the Kent farmland on his right, as he drove, had not been replaced by business parks and high rise flats. He wondered just how long that would remain the case. The A2 turned into the M2 and his speed picked up again until he had to turn onto the A249 towards Sheppey.

He found the site fairly easily. It was a little north-east of a small hamlet called Harty and was on remote farmland. The more remote the better for his friend Pearson who didn't like the modern world that much and never carried a mobile phone with him. Nevertheless Jim knew he'd be on site. He even preferred to sleep in his battered old tent rather than a local hotel or B&B. The bean counters at the University of Kent where he was head of History at Canterbury loved him as he never exceeded his budget for any of the digs he worked on. Jim parked on the road within sight of the excavation and immediately spotted Pearson in his familiar poncho. Pearson looked up and recognised the black Lincoln and waved and Anderson moved warily over the ground in his ox blood coloured boots. There were several areas marked off by tape almost like a crime scene on TV which he avoided and found his way over to where Pearson was supervising a quartet of his students who were helping on the dig. He was a small man in his sixties with long salt and pepper hair that was tied in a ponytail with what looked like a long red shoelace. Under the poncho he wore brown dungarees over a very thick green jumper and his trouser legs were tucked firmly into a pair of wellies that had seen better days. He shook Jim's hand with his own that was covered with a latex glove.

"Well, this is a pleasant surprise! How are you old chap?" enthused Pearson.

"Very good Stuart, I thought I'd come down to check out your latest site and to ask your opinion on something the son of a friend found. I'm pretty sure it's Saxon and you are always at the top of my list when it comes to that period."

"Lovely to be so highly regarded, dear boy, shall we retire to the only pub within miles? It's just down the road in the direction you're pointed."

"Sounds good, hopefully they are still serving food," said Jim, feeling his stomach beginning to rumble. He really fancied a pint of the local ale too.

They walked towards Jim's huge car and Pearson changed his wellies for an ancient pair of carpet slippers he always kept in a pocket of his work clothes and deposited the wellies in the boot of the Lincoln.

"Some things never change," laughed Jim. "You are definitely the weirdest man I've ever met and you can do with a new pair of slippers."

"I'm always prepared in case some nice chap turns up to take me to the pub. And haven't I just been proven right? The landlord doesn't like wellies in his bar which is a bit strange in a farming community but he does seem like a bit of a snob."

They drove the few hundred yards to the pub. The small car park was deserted as the lunchtime trade had gone. It was a large, white sixteenth century building with a barn that had been converted into the main dining area. They decided to stick to the bar and sat at a table and Jim ordered beer battered cod with tartare sauce, chips and minted peas from the heavy oak counter for them both while getting the drinks. Pearson had a large gin and tonic while Jim chose a beer recommended by the pretty young girl behind the workbench. Jim immediately had lustful thoughts about the thin, dark haired girl who was young enough to be his daughter or maybe even granddaughter at a push.

"So, tell me about the dig," said Jim as they waited for their late lunch.

"Well, as you already know it's definitely a Saxon site. By the look of the pottery we found so far the village was established not long after the Romans vacated the area and was probably one of the first good sized Saxon settlements in England. We've mapped out the remains of the fence that surrounded the village and already found the Great Hall and a couple of smaller buildings. It is in the perfect position. Not too far from the coast so they had access to fishing, yet far enough away that they were shielded from the coastal weather by the surrounding forest. Plenty of access to fresh water and also wild game. It really could be a significant find and we think it pre-dates Sutton Hoo by a couple of centuries and the Canterbury sites by about a hundred years," Pearson beamed with pride.

"It really would be a great find. How was it discovered?"

"Usual thing. The farmer trying to rotate the soil a bit deeper than normal found pottery and a few pieces of metalwork, mainly brooches. A friend suggested he send them to the Canterbury campus and they fell into my lap as usual. I'd almost given up the thought of another dig as I'm getting on a bit but this came at the perfect time for me. It could be a magnificent last hurrah before I retire if things work out like I hope. The appearances in the odd documentary will supplement my pension and I may even become a Youtube star," he joked.

"Brilliant. A bit like a Saxon farewell for their king," smiled Jim.

"I'm not quite ready for a burial mound, dear boy." They both laughed at the prospect. "Tell me about the other reason you're here."

Jim fished the amulet from his pocket and passed it to Pearson. "The son of a friend was out walking and fell over a tree root and this was exposed. Fairly near where I live, in fact. I'm pretty sure it's Saxon and may be dated around 450."

"Well, you are spot on with the date - I'd say 450 to 470 to be exact. You've deciphered the text on it I take it?"

"Yes, 'I will return' and 'six will die', Lars Lind helped with that. I have a theory that it belonged to Kendra Watkin."

"Very good. Used by a witch to invoke eternal life and immortality. There would be a need to make six sacrifices after the witch was dead. The face on the reverse side would be the demon conjured to perform the sacrifices. You never met the ex-wife did you? Remarkable likeness. It's interesting that you think it was dear old Mother Watkin, obviously she was the most well known witch where this was found and it's a complete mystery what happened to her. It's entirely possible this was hers. She would have hidden it somewhere and when it was found the demon would awake and do it's dastardly deeds. Strictly speaking if this has only just been found by that friend of yours then the demon hasn't had a chance yet. That's if demons exist which I very much doubt, but wouldn't it be interesting if they did, think of the havoc and revenge you could summon if you had control of one, similar to the Jewish Golem. I believe the demon may have been known by the name Anrok. It was one of those they would evoke specifically for revenge."

On the way back from Salisbury Mark and Nat stopped at a small town to relax and make the most of their day. They found a tiny art gallery sandwiched between a pound shop and a pizza restaurant and ventured inside to browse and admire the work of local artists. There were the usual landscapes and sunsets as well as a lot of wildlife paintings. Nat particularly loved one of a pair of otters but was put off by the price tag. Some paintings were totally bizarre and made no sense to either of them. Neither understood abstracts and preferred the more traditional type of painting, ones you could actually work out what the artist was trying to paint. There were plenty of cartoon characters in vivid colours and a few still lifes. Mark really liked the fantasy stuff by one local artist in particular, lots of fairies, toadstools and a few of Stonehenge and other standing stones. He wondered if she had ever been to Marsham. The most impressive piece of art was a bronze sculpture of a strutting lion that was going for a little more than the price of a brand new Mercedes. They turned a corner in the gallery and Mark froze. Facing them was a dark and disturbing picture of a woman screaming in what looked like anger rather than pain or fright. She was portrayed from the waist up dressed in black with long black hair and glowing red eyes. The background was patches of red and yellow in very broad strokes and blurred. Mark thought it looked like flames lapping around the woman. The picture was framed and had a small plaque at the bottom centre. It read: *Retribution by Dominic Brand.* It really gave Mark a chill as he studied the face of the woman. Was she being punished for something or was she the one wreaking retribution on someone else? Did she set the fire? Mark suggested they leave and find a pub.

They found a place about fifty yards down the high street called the George and Dragon. It was a large former coaching inn built in the eighteenth century and sported a giant arch at the end of the building which led to a courtyard at the back that was used for parking and deliveries. The front entrance was flanked on either side by metal railings with rather lethal looking spikes on each of the uprights. Mark led the way up three well worn stone steps and into the foyer. There was a dining area to the left but they turned right into the bar, He ordered a large scotch for himself and Nat asked for a dry white wine and they sat at a table next to a window that looked out onto a newsagents next to a funeral director. Mark was reminded of Steve and Kim's need for their help with the funeral.

"I need this," Mark said as he took a gulp of his drink, relishing the burning sensation as the liquid sank into his chest. "That picture almost freaked me out. It was like a panic attack."

"I didn't like it either but it didn't really give me an intense feeling like it did with you. I suppose different people see different things in art. Van Gogh is apparently one of the greatest painters ever but I've never seen the attraction myself. Give me a seascape of the Battle of Trafalgar any day."

"Maybe one day I will," grinned Mark, already feeling a little calmer than he had been a few minutes earlier, the amber fluid doing it's thing.

They chatted about their day in Salisbury and the amazing sights inside the cathedral and decided if they were in the area in future they'd spend more time in the museum. They'd been to the Ashmolean in Oxford before and regretted not giving themselves two days to fully immerse themselves in the experience. They only viewed the ground floor and part of the next one when they had run out of time. Nat suggested they visit again the next day before heading home and Mark thought that was a great idea. There was so much there to see. They still wouldn't have time for everything, Mark thought it would take four or five full days and that didn't even include the exhibits hidden away from the public in the vaults.

Mark was just about to check to find a bed and breakfast near to the museum and make it a two day stay when his mobile started ringing. He saw on the display that it was Jim. Mark answered the call and Jim's sounded like he was in a wind tunnel.

"Evening Mark, sorry for the sound effects but I'm outside a pub and it's a little blustery. The locals have descended from who knows where as this place is pretty bleak and deserted to be honest. It's a little noisy indoors."

"Hi Jim, we're actually inside a pub and it's very quiet at the moment. I assume you have news?"

"Just a little. My friend narrowed the date to between 450 and 470 and is convinced it was taken from a large standing stone to be used in a pagan ritual to give the witch immortality. There would have been six sacrifices for the rite to be completed and the face on the back would be the demon conjured to make those sacrifices. He says the name of the demon could have been Anrok, a specialist in revenge apparently. I did a little research and he was indeed a nasty piece of work, one of the worst in fact. The interesting thing is that the ritual failed for some reason otherwise the amulet would have been destroyed. He agrees that Kendra Watkin is a prime candidate to have tried to perform the rite. I'm going to spend the night here at the pub and tomorrow will drive back and dig up, pun intended, all I can about dear old Kendra and call you in the next couple of days."

"Sounds good. We're spending the next day or two in Oxford at the Ashmolean Museum and then heading home. We had a break-in at the flat while we were sleeping and needed to get away. I need to call my folks in a minute to ask if we can stay at their place for a few days until I can rent another flat."

"I'm sorry to hear that. It must have been terrifying for you. Was there much taken?"

"Nothing. But they were searching for something. Draws and cupboards were turned out but nothing was missing as far as we can tell. They left a note saying 'give it back'. The police seem to think that as I have no idea what it means it could be they ransacked the wrong flat. We're just relieved we weren't attacked in our sleep."

"Staying at your parents house is probably a good idea. The intruder or intruders may not realise it was the wrong place and could be back, so better safe than sorry. That note is a bit of a mystery. I wonder what they were after. Probably connected to the low life drug dealers in the area. Maybe someone ran off with a stash or something? Anyway, I'm freezing out here so I'll talk to you in a couple of days. Look after yourself."

"You too Jim, get yourself something large and warming from the bar. Speak soon."

Mark hung up and gave Nat the news from Jim. They were getting hungry again and decided to soak their drinks up with a meal in the restaurant in the other side of the building. They both chose steak in peppercorn sauce with mash, green beans and peas and followed that with a gorgeous strawberry gateau and vanilla ice cream and then left to return to Marlborough for the night.

The woman rose early. Sleep had brought bad dreams of serpents and demons. She was in her early forties and quite tall and dressed in a lengthy dark linen dress with her top half covered in a dull red tunic. She had very dark, almost black, eyes and long black hair tied in a loose tail at the back and was very beautiful. She staggered outside her hut deep in the woods and winced as she looked at the sun. Her hut was made of wood with a thatched roof and was in good condition compared to some in the nearby village. There was a small clearing a few feet away ringed by a pen made from stout branches. Inside the pen her pigs grunted as she approached with a bowl of bones and vegetable scraps from the thick rabbit stew she had made the previous evening. The villagers paid her in vegetables and cloth for her services as a healer, although many regarded her as a witch. She knew that she was safe from the villagers as they accepted that she had the power for evil and revenge as well as good but she rarely used the dark side of her abilities. Even the local lord was wary of her and left her alone because he still believed in the pagan ways. The only real danger in the woods were the wolves but she regarded them more of a protection than a threat. She threw the contents of the bowl into the pen and the three pigs competed for the scraps in a frenzy. It would soon be time to slaughter one of them with winter approaching. She'd salt the meat and store it in a small hole next to the hut which was covered with a layer of branches and leaves to keep it cool. When the snows came the pigs would be moved into her hut to provide a little warmth for her and to prevent them freezing to death in the open. She never visited the village and had no wish to. The sick and injured were always brought to her through the wood. The sick would usually stay a few days until they recovered. Rarely one of them died but the majority were cured by her. Her reputation was second to none as a healer but sometimes even she could do nothing.

She heard the crackle and rustling of the fallen leaves as someone approached. She turned in that direction and saw a young girl making her way through the trees carrying a small linen bag in one hand while gingerly holding the other arm against her flat chest. She was very slight with blond hair and striking blue eyes and was very pretty beneath the dirt on her face and was dressed in little more than rags. The girl was very nervous as it was the first time she needed to visit.

"Are you Mother Watkin?" she stuttered with fear.

"I am child, you need healing by the look of you. No need to be afraid of me."

"Yes Mother, I dropped a pan of boiling water and some fell on my arm. I have brought you payment to help me, it is all my father could spare."

The girl handed the bag to the older woman who looked inside. There were two cabbages and a few parsnips.

"This will do. Villagers have told me the crops this year have been sparse. Come into the hut and let me see what you've done."

The girl followed tentatively and entered the dark home of Mother Watkin. She sat on a small bed while Watkin crouched and started to mix the ingredients for the poultice she was going to apply. Watkin chopped garlic and added yeast, bark from a Yew tree and a few other herbs and shaved slivers from a root with a large sharp knife. She then added honey and mixed them all together while closing her eyes and mumbling a phrase over and over again. After around five minutes she leaned over to the girl and plastered the burns with the cool mixture and then wet a cloth from a nearby wooden bowl and wrapped that over the whole area then tied the cloth around the thin arm at the top and bottom with two long, thin leather thongs.

"Leave this on for seven days. Tell your father you must rest and not work in the fields. You may do domestic chores but do not get the wrapping wet."

"Thank you Mother. I am most grateful to you."

"What is your name girl?" asked the healer.

"My name is Wilda, daughter of Ware."

"Yes, I know him. He's been here himself. You are welcome to visit whenever you please."

"Thank you, I will come again. I would be most happy if you allowed me to learn from you."

"Yes. I feel you have a little power to heal. I'd be happy to teach you. I have no child of my own to pass on my knowledge."

Wilda smiled and turned towards the woods and sang to herself as she returned to the village a little over two miles away. Mother Watkin lit a fire close to the front of her hut and brewed a drink made from bark and berries while she sliced one of the cabbages to add to the stew pot. She liked the girl, Wilda, and wondered how much she'd be able to teach her. Being a healer was a good life. Respected and sometimes feared and always a supply of vegetables to be gained for her work. She smiled to herself. It pleased her to help people.

Saturday April 25th

Before Mark and Nat left for Oxford, Mark called his parents and asked if they could spend a few days at their place as they really didn't feel comfortable returning to Mark's flat after the break-in. Ellie said they could stay as long as they liked and she would prepare Mark's old room for them. Mark said they would be there sometime late afternoon on Sunday and Ellie said there would be a nice meal waiting for them. She'd already picked up a nice joint of pork from the butchers in Marsham village and would do something special with it for them. Mark told her about where they had been for the last couple of days and had plenty of pictures to show them from their travels. Ellie said she couldn't wait to see them and had always loved the cathedral at Salisbury but had never been to the museum there.

They left the hotel just after their morning meal for the trip to Oxford. Mark had already booked a bed and breakfast near the Ashmolean for one night so the plan was to spend most of the day researching the collection of Saxon artifacts and then maybe go back again in the morning for some general browsing of the art there. They travelled east towards Newbury and then veered north to Oxford. The whole journey only took an hour to the huge car park on the outskirts and then they took a bus into the city centre and got off near the B&B. Mrs Parker was a tall, prim looking woman who wouldn't look out of place in a Victorian school. She showed them to their room on the first floor and proceeded to tell them the house rules. Mark left their cases in the room and immediately wanted to get to the museum which was about half a mile from the house. On their way they stopped to pick up a couple of coffees in waxed cardboard cups. The brew was very strong and needed topping up with milk after a couple of sips. As they walked towards the museum they were amazed by all the people begging on the streets, not just buskers but teens actually lying down on the pavement with a placard and a begging bowl.

By the time they reached the front entrance to the giant building they had finished their coffees and shrugged off any guilt about not donating to the countless beggars. It wasn't as if either were particularly well paid and Nat wouldn't be paid for the time off this week. They entered through the main doors between four tall pillars and took a quick look around the ground floor with all the statues and objects in a myriad of glass cases. After a while they asked a member of staff where the Saxon exhibits were and were directed to the second floor. The majority of the artifacts seemed to be brooches and rings but what really caught Mark's eye was a display of ceremonial knives used for pagan ritual sacrifices.

He could picture the scene where the throat of a pig, goat or ox would be sliced open and the blood collected in bowls, the head cut off and buried face down and then a feast of the meat, cooked on a spit. Some of these rituals were performed at the burial of an important member of the tribe but mostly they were to pacify their gods like the chief one Woden and Tiw who was their god of war.

They took their time looking at the rest of the collections on the second floor. The Alfred Jewel was a particular highlight of the later Saxon period as well as the Minster Lovell Jewel, both pieces with their gold sparkling beneath the lights of the exhibit. There was an excellent display of Japanese art including an impressive collection of porcelain and an amazing Samurai suit of armour from the seventeenth century. Mark wondered what it would be like to fight in such a bulky ceremonial suit and was thankful he'd never have to find out.

There was also a good Chinese section from almost eight hundred years earlier than the Japanese one. Paintings of dragons dominated, all in rich colours, mainly blues and reds, as well as a large statue of Buddha from the thirteenth century and a lot of glazed ceramics. They finished off their afternoon with a tour of the various galleries housing French, Italian, Dutch, Flemish and German paintings and other artwork. Nat particularly loved the Dutch and Flemish still-life. Later at the gift shop she bought a framed print of Still Life With Oysters by Jacob Foppens Van Es for £80 that would be produced and delivered to her mum's house while she stayed at Jack and Ellie's home. She would have bought one or two more but money was a little tight at the moment. Mark found a print of Stonehenge by William Turner of Oxford, often confused with the more famous Turner because their styles were so similar. He chose a medium framed copy and paid £110 - this would be a wedding anniversary present for his parents who would be celebrating their thirtieth very soon.

The pair left shortly afterwards and found a nearby cafe and sat outside on the terrace. They watched the world go by. The hustle and bustle of a typical Saturday afternoon. Mark much preferred the more sedate weekends in rural Hertfordshire. His phone rang loudly.

"Hi Jim," he said.

"Good evening Mark," said Jim excitedly. "I've been looking at the depiction of the demon on the reverse of the amulet and saw something remarkable. There are Runic symbols hidden in the face."

"Really? Any idea what they mean?"

"So far I've found thorn, yew and birch but there are other symbols there. The face is part of the incantation to invoke eternal life somehow. I should have more by tomorrow."
"That's great, we're on our way back in the morning, can we stop off and have a look?"

"Of course, I'll look forward to it. I'm now entirely convinced that the demon was Anrok. He is thought to have been pretty ruthless when invoked."
"I'm glad he is only a myth, I wouldn't like to get involved with anything like that," said Mark."

"See you tomorrow then."

"Has Jim found out more?" asked Nat.

"Yes. He says there are Runic symbols hidden in the face of that demon on the amulet, could be important. We need to nip in to see him on our way back."

"This thing just gets creepier by the day. Everything just seems odd at the moment, Steve's accident, that guy from your office, the break-in."

"Well they say bad luck comes in threes so hopefully that's the end of it," smiled Mark.

Jim was feeling pretty pleased with himself for noticing the symbols in the representation of Anrok. This must have been some very serious magic the thought. He was no expert on Runes but he easily deciphered the inscription around face of the amulet with the help of an online Runic to English translator he'd found. On further reading he'd found out that not only were specific letters present in their alphabet but also symbols for whole words, like Pagan emojis he thought amusedly. There were hidden symbols all over the face. Eyes, nose and ears mostly but also some on the horns of the creature. It would take time to find and decipher everything. He thought the real message was not the inscription on the front but hidden in the demonic carving on the reverse, a bit like the hidden things in the paintings of Da Vinci. He imagined himself presenting a documentary on this find on the History Channel in a few months.

Mother Watkin had been spending a lot of time with Wilda. She liked the girl and as she was without child thought that Wilda could learn from her and would make a good healer. Wilda had an affinity with nature, that was very clear, and that was a good start. She quickly learnt about the various herbs, roots and fungi that Watkin used for her cures and poultices. The girl was very bright and absorbed the knowledge willingly and with ease. Watkin soon became proud of Wilda as if she were her own offspring. Sometimes she let Wilda mix and apply a poultice for some minor ailments and was happy with the results. It wasn't magic, just medicine. The magic would come later.

There was barely any trace of the burn on Wilda's arm, healed in seven days just as Mother Watkin had said. Wilda longed for the day when she could heal as well as the white witch.

Watkin and Wilda were enjoying a brew made from bark and ginger. Wilda had prepared the drink which she did daily as part of her duties. She thought of herself as an apprentice now. She loved learning about nature and how to heal people and her father had agreed to her spending time with Watkin and learning from her. He knew that his own status would rise with a healer in the family. Wilda spent less time working on the farm but he knew that what she learnt from the healer would be worth the extra work for him and his other children.

"You learn quickly child," said Watkin as they crouched next to the small fire outside the entrance to the hut. "After your chores I will teach you how to mend bones. First you must collect wood for the fire and the usual roots and berries. I have a rabbit to skin and make ready for the pot."

"Yes, Mother Watkin. I look forward to the day when you have taught me all you know," said the young girl.

"I may not teach you all I know, that depends on you."

"Yes mother."

"You've heard the villagers talking of my dark magic?"

"Yes, they say that no one should cross you because you can make bad things happen. They say even Lord Machen will not harm you or demand tribute. They say he is scared of you."

"He has been advised by many people who have witnessed my power. It has been ten years since I've had to use it to punish anyone but people have long memories."

"What did you do to them Mother?" asked the girl.

"All I will say is that some men who worked the land for the Machen family tried to take advantage of me and they paid for it. No one who witnessed their final days will ever forget."

"My father wouldn't tell me when I asked him."

"He knew some of them, he is wise to stay silent, and you should not be asking him of me, you ask me instead and I will answer if I can and if you are ready to hear."

"Yes mother, I'm sorry."

"Now attend to your chores, there is much to do today and I want you safe at home before dark."

Wilda took several leather straps with which to tie the twigs for the fire and a large cloth sack for the roots and herbs and whatever berries she could find. Mother Watkin entered the hut and brought out the rabbit she had caught overnight in one of her snares. She was lucky that every two or three nights one of her traps would give her something for the pot. She waved the dead rabbit in the air and said a few words of thanks to Woden and proceeded to gut it and then skin it with her small knife. She severed the head and feet with an axe and wrapped the body of the rabbit in wet cloth before she rubbed it with salt and herbs. She then picked the head up and moved to the edge of the wood and buried it face down as part of the ritual. The rabbit skin would be added to a winter shawl she was making for Wilda. The thin clothes she wore wouldn't be much protection for the girl as she walked through the freezing woods when the snows came.

Sunday April 26th

The next morning Mark and Nat left the bed and breakfast and took the bus to the park where they'd left the Jaguar. The previous evening they had been idly browsing the internet about the Oxford area and read about the Harcourt Arboretum. They had some time to spare before they needed to arrive at Jim's house so decided to visit the park before the drive back. They needed to relax before the new week started with a return to work and helping Kim organise Steve's funeral as well as trying to find a flat for Mark to move into although that wasn't a priority at the moment. Mark knew his parents would be happy for them to stay for as long as they needed.

They headed south and a little over thirty minutes later easily found the entrance to the arboretum and parked near the ticket office just inside. They walked into the park hand in hand and strolled around, just unwinding in the peace of the Oxfordshire countryside. The trail took them through the Acer glade and then the coppice. Nat could faintly smell her favourite flowers and they quickly found the bluebell wood where they stood and breathed in the aroma. It was very intoxicating inhaling the almost oily perfume of the blooms. They continued to walk through the gardens, marvelling at the different types of trees all in the same area. They saw beds of daffodils, their heads swaying in the light breeze and an array of wildlife including hares and a peacock. On the way back towards the car park there was a meadow to their left, lush grassland covered with wildflowers of mainly yellow mixed with patches of white. Nat gasped as she spotted a fox about a hundred yards away watching them warily. She pointed to it and Mark saw it but his attention went beyond that to the woods maybe half a mile in the distance. He thought he could see a dark shape a dozen or so feet inside the tree line. He stared at the unmoving figure for what seemed like minutes until a mist started to develop further in the woods and swallowed the apparition until it disappeared. He could swear he heard words forming in the breeze. It sounded like 'give it back' but it could have been something else. The phrase had been in his head since the break-in. He practically pulled Nat down the path towards the exit. He just couldn't understand what was happening to him. Was the figure real? Was the mist even real? He was going to ask Nat if she saw anything but didn't want to alarm her. If it was his imagination then he'd keep it to himself and put it down the the stress of the last week. Could he be developing some sort of psychosis?

They left the park and made their way towards Jim's house, Deep Purple blaring from the car speakers. Mark tried to forget about the eerie experience at the arboretum. These last few days were supposed to de-stress him after the awful week they'd had but he still felt tense and wary. He really didn't feel like going back to work in the morning but he had to pay the bills somehow. He wished he could just wake up in the morning and everything would turn out to be a dream instead of a living nightmare. No break-in, no suicide of Paul and Steve would still be alive. His head felt like there was a low level buzzing inside. He'd never had to deal with so much stress in his life before. The Oxfordshire countryside sped past his window as he guided the Jag down the M40. The sun shone down from a clear spring sky and dazzled him slightly so he reached into the centre console for his sunglasses and put them on. The buzzing in his head faded a little and he felt more confident and relaxed as he drove. Nat was doing something on her phone, he assumed she was on Facebook or texting her mum. He didn't mind, he didn't really want conversation at that moment. He was quite happy listening to the music and concentrating on the road.

He pulled up in front of Jim's house just after two o'clock. Jim's study was in the same unruly state it was the previous Sunday, maybe even slightly worse, but he thought Jim probably knew exactly where everything was. An untidy workspace didn't usually mean an untidy mind and Jim seemed very intelligent and a little eccentric but most of all he was enthusiastic. Jim made a pot of tea and placed the tray on a fairly clear corner of his desk and poured into three mismatched cups.

"So, as I said yesterday I found the Runic symbols for thorn, yew and birch in the face of the demon." He held up a small card with runes printed on it and pointed to the right eye of the face. "Here you can see that eye is made up of the mark for birch tree and an ear fashioned from the design for yew. I cleaned up the amulet even more last night and found water, fire and journey as well."

"That's amazing," said Nat, feeling more at ease with Jim after being a bit wary on the first visit.

"So what does it all mean?" Mark asked, "You said it was a ritual or spell for immortality but how would it actually work?"

"Well, as you know the Runic inscription indicated that there would have to be six sacrifices the witch needed to make. Normally in Pagan rituals they would have used animals but for something as important as this I'd say they were human sacrifices. This amulet is very unusual, unique I'd say. Pretty potent magic was needed to give someone eternal life and according to Stuart it didn't work which is why this stone still exists, so either there is no such thing as magic or someone or something prevented it from being completed."

"That sounds so creepy," said Nat, "I wonder if it was really possible to give yourself eternal life, what if you were severely injured or lost a leg or went blind? Imagine being like that for eternity?"

"Not a pleasant thought, I'd say," chuckled Jim. "I've also been thinking more about the identity of our witch. I'm pretty convinced it was indeed Kendra Watkin. There is just no other witch from this area or anywhere near that was considered to have that much power. From what scholars of the period, myself included, know about her was that she was mainly known as a healer or if you were either brave or foolish you would call her a white witch. Like all witches there would be a side to her that you wouldn't want to upset. She would have had knowledge of dark magic. She wouldn't have been liked but she certainly would have been respected. In those days a minor infection could have been fatal and she probably saved many lives. She would have lived alone, well out the way of the nearest village but that suited both parties. She would have been paid in goods for her services and also lived off the land. She was essential to the community although none would want to be in her company for too long if they could help it."

"Sounds like an interesting life," said Mark.

"I suppose to her it was just normal, she came from a long line of healers so wouldn't think anything of it. It was her destiny. I don't know if she had any offspring to pass her knowledge on to. There normally would be. Maybe the reason she wanted immortality was because there was no child or children to pass on the legacy?"

"Something intriguing happened at an art gallery we visited near Salisbury," said Mark. "I found myself face to face with a painting that gave me a strange feeling. It was of a screaming woman and I think she was being burnt to death although she looked angry instead of in pain. I just got the feeling it was connected to the amulet in some way although the area is completely different. It was by an artist called Dominic Brand and called *Retribution*."

"Sounds familiar."

Jim sat at his desk and fired up his PC. After a minute he Googled Dominic Brand and like most modern artists there was a website displaying his works and a rather long, probably self-penned, biography. "I thought I recognised the name, he was actually born locally in Marsham but moved away to Wiltshire when he was a child. He's not really famous but which artist is until they die? I quite like his style, sometimes a little dark for my tastes though."

He clicked on the screen and turned the monitor so that Mark could see the screen, "Is that the one?"

"Yes, that's it! Do you see what I mean?"

"Very interesting," said Jim. "Bit of a coincidence that you found this and it turns out he is from around here, almost as if you were meant to find it. There is a number for him on the site, you could give him a ring tomorrow and try and find out his inspiration for the painting." Jim found a scrap of paper and copied the number for Mark on what was an old petrol receipt.

"Thanks, I will," Mark said as he pushed the paper into a small pocket inside his phone case. "I'll call you if I find anything interesting."

Mark guided the Jag gingerly around the one track lanes which led to his parents house. They arrived after three-thirty and were greeted at the door by Jack and Ellen. Mark took the bags upstairs to his old room and left them at the foot of the bed and went down and joined the others. Nat was already loading the pictures from her camera onto Jack's PC and setting up the slide show program. Before they sat around the large monitor Jack poured drinks for everyone and they all settled down for the show. Jack and Ellie had been to Stonehenge and Salisbury Cathedral in the past and reminisced about their own visits. They hadn't been to the museum almost next door to the Cathedral though and enjoyed the pictures of the exhibits there. The Ashmolean was well known to them as their university days were in Oxford and they actually met at the museum while looking at the coin collections.

The slide show progressed to the arboretum and the many pictures of both flora and fauna from Nat's camera.

"That's strange," said Ellie. "I thought I saw a figure out of the corner of my eye in a couple of snaps but when I looked closer there was nothing there."

"Probably a trick of the light or a shadow," replied Jack. "I didn't notice anything."

The slide show continued. Mark stayed silent but as the images got nearer to where he saw his own dark figure he started to get nervous. Would Ellie see something in the same place he had? Mark took a large swallow of his scotch and hoped not. Next were a pair of nice photos of the fox they had seen and that was it! Nothing after the fox but Mark was sure Nat had taken more pictures after that before he hurried her out of the park. He breathed a sigh of relief but was also confused. What happened to them?

"So that's it," smiled Nat. "I really loved our trip, especially the Cathedral. It was all a bit last minute after what happened at the flat but we made the best of it. Thank you so much for letting us stay here for a few days, I really appreciate it. We just couldn't spend another night there."

"It's our pleasure, and you know you are always welcome and can stay as long as you want," said Ellie, and Jack nodded in agreement.

"I don't suppose you've heard anything from the police yet? asked Jack.

"Nothing yet," answered Mark. "I doubt they'll catch anyone. There were no fingerprints left, no physical evidence at all. I'm not even sure they believed us to be honest."

"Well, honest is exactly what you two are," said Jack. "I'm sure there are some attention seekers who would stage a break-in to spice up their boring lives or even some who would fake a robbery for an insurance scam but that isn't you."

They played a game of Trivial Pursuit which Ellie won easily. She even got her cricket question right, much to the chagrin of Jack who prided himself as a cricket expert. A smile of satisfaction was on Ellie's face and she stuck her tongue out at Jack on her way to the kitchen to cook the meal. An hour later she emerged and told the others that her new recipe was ready and smelled wonderful. It was the first time she had tried Pork fillet with smoked paprika and piquillo peppers with a side salad and she was very pleased at how it turned out. Not only did it smell lovely it looked great too and she couldn't wait for everyone to try it. As expected everyone loved it as they washed it down with a dry white wine.

"That was amazing, thank you mum," said Mark. "Not too fattening either. I won't need to go for a walk later to burn it all off."

"We have golden milk and turmeric ice cream with blueberries for dessert," chuckled Ellie.

"Maybe I will then," he laughed.

After the meal and with Mark feeling very fat he and Jack saw to the washing up as usual with the help of a single malt and chatted mainly about sport and arranged to get out for a round of golf at the local course the next Saturday. Ellie and Nat were in the front room watching The Sound Of Music and Jack rolled his eyes every time the ladies sang along with the songs. Jack suggested moving to the patio for another scotch and they sat there for the next hour enjoying the spring weather and the rather nice single malt. They watched the birds and butterflies flitting from the flowers and bushes that lined the large garden. There were several Orange Tip butterflies feeding on the nectar from the Hyacinths and Pansies to their left and the birds chirped busily.

When their film was over Ellie and Nat came out to join them still singing the songs and giggling like schoolgirls. It was just what Nat needed after the trials of the last week and she looked a lot more relaxed. The wine they were drinking during the film probably had an effect too because they were on their second bottle. They all sat admiring the garden which was Ellie's passion now that she had retired. Ellie pointed out to Nat what she had done recently and her plans for the area in the near future. Her next project would be a herb garden as she used a lot in her cooking and insisted that home grown parsley, basil, coriander and rosemary and a few others would taste better than supermarket bought ones and she wouldn't be wasting any either, she could just cut what she needed.

Mark told Ellie about the research Jim was doing and all they had found out between them and also recounted the strange feeling he got when he saw that painting by Dominic Brand. Ellie said she knew the name and vaguely remembered a bit of gossip about him from years ago. Something to do with him being an outcast as a child and the family leaving the village.

Mark said he'd go for a walk so went up to change into some old jogging bottoms, sweatshirt and trainers that he always kept at his parents house as he often had a walk after lunch. The scotch made him feel a little light headed too so needed to get out and blow away some cobwebs. He set off down the lane at a brisk pace with music coming from his phone though cheap wired earphones he kept in the car as a spare as his earbuds were at his flat. Gary Moore's haunting *The Loner* sounded a bit tinny from the earphones but it was better than nothing. He'd have to get another cheap set of earbuds just for walks from his parents house if it took a while to find a new flat . He just couldn't walk without music in his head. He could entirely switch his brain off and just walk without thinking of the daily burdens of work and he needed to try and get the last week out of his mind. It was a week since Steve's accident and he knew he'd have to call Kim later. The lanes around the house weren't busy, they rarely were. His usual lap took him out into the country and farmland. He passed several fields with an assortment of cows and sheep and as he passed close to a farm he was almost overwhelmed by the smell of the fresh manure the farmer was spreading over one of the fields he used for crops, probably corn or kale. He turned right into a short lane and just avoided a cyclist flying around the corner in the opposite direction without a care or the sense to think there may be the odd car or tractor heading his way. Cyclists always annoyed him. He loved to walk along the towpath of the local canal but there were so many idiots on bikes rushing past him and he was tempted just to stick an elbow out and send them into the water. He smiled at the idea of a spandex clad moron getting a good dowsing.

In the centre of the field to his left was a small dell with trees growing from it. A depression in the ground that was allegedly made by a Lancaster jettisoning a bomb that failed to drop over Germany that they were desperate to release before landing at a nearby airfield during the last war. Mark used to play in that dell when he was a kid. For some reason someone had dumped an old, light blue Ford Anglia in the dell and he always wondered how it got there and why but it made great cover during games of 'war' with his friends. The car was rusted and eaten away in patches and getting cut on the rotten bodywork meant a trip to Dr. Furlong and a tetanus jab. He decided to climb the gate of the field and take a walk to the dell across the ploughed surface. When he got there he gingerly squeezed through a fence made from two strands of rusty barbed wire and slowly descended the side of the depression. Memories of his youth came flooding back, friends like Wally, Chalky and Little Mike all played in that dell with him. They were all the same age as him and were all at school together from nursery up to secondary school. All three had moved away in the last five or six years like a lot of people from the village and Mark missed them. Wally was up in Manchester working for a firm of solicitors. Chalky worked abroad in the Saudi oil fields and Little Mike had set up his own plumbing business near Gloucester.

The old Ford was still there and Mark wondered if it always would be, like a local monument, a modern version of the stones at Marsham. There was very little of the bodywork left, just dark brown brittle metal that would probably collapse if he put any weight on it. The seats were just springs and all the glass was missing. Mark wasn't sure if any kids ever played here anymore with the current trend of over-protective parents scared of their little darlings getting hurt but then again Mark rarely saw groups of children playing anywhere now. Probably too busy playing on game consoles or their mobile phones. He was always out playing football at every opportunity until he reached sixteen and discovered beer and girls and even then he found time for a kick about with his mates and a proper game for the local team on a Sunday. One thing he didn't miss was a game on a frozen council maintained pitch in the depths of winter where if a ball hit you it felt like a sledge hammer and you thought you were crippled for life. He loved playing until his accident stopped any sort of exercise except walking and some light weight training. He supposed it could have been worse as he could be in a wheelchair for life if the injury had been any worse.

The air temperature felt like it had dropped a few degrees and Mark shivered. Maybe it was the thought of those frozen pitches making him feel that way. He supposed that as he was thirty feet down in the dell that the temperature would be colder than ground level anyway but he realised it really was getting colder. Cold as the grave as the saying went. He looked up and saw there was a thick fog rolling in from his right. It was moving slowly down the side of the dell and he felt like there was a

cold lump of granite in his stomach. Not much scared him, cancer and wasps mainly, but he was beginning to feel very uneasy and certainly didn't want to try and find his way out of the dell in a blanket of fog. He knew he would probably panic a bit if he didn't get out very soon. He started to climb the slope directly opposite from where the fog was descending, digging his feet into the soft earth and grabbing at exposed tree roots to pull himself up. His feet slipped a couple of times but managed to keep his balance and almost did a backwards somersault when one of the roots he was heaving himself up with snapped. He got to the top and had laid his hand on top of one of the wooden posts that held the barbed fire fence and looked back. The entire floor of the dell was covered in the thick fog and he saw the dark shape in it, hovering above the old Ford. It was then that he really did start to panic. He tried to jump the top strand of barbed wire instead of trying to wiggle between the two lines of metal but his wrist caught on the upper wire and ripped a shallow but long gash up to his forearm.
'Give it back!' The words invaded his mind or maybe he heard them again?
He screamed more in fear than pain and managed to untangle himself and get over the fence and then he ran for the first time in over four years. Pure adrenaline pumped through his system as he pounded away across the uneven field to the gate. He vaulted the three bar iron gate and looked back. Most of the field was enveloped in the hazy gloom. It was then that the pain in his back hit him and the world turned black.

Mother Watkin woke to to sound of shouts and the noise of twigs and bushes being snapped and crushed. She wearily rose and opened the door of her hut and was confronted by an angry crowd.

"Where is she?" implored Wilda's father. "What have you done to her?"

"I've done nothing, Wilda left at the usual time yesterday."

"She didn't arrive home!" He pushed past Watkin and peered into the hut.

"She's not here!" said Watkin angrily. "Get out of there, you haven't been invited!"

"For your sake you should wish nothing has happened to her!" he shouted.

"And for yours too, you know not to cross me, Ware. Do not accuse me because you know what would happen."

Ware scowled at her as the mob drifted away to continue the search for

Wilda. Watkin was concerned. She liked the girl very much and if anything had happened to her there would be trouble for the healer despite the fear the villagers held. She knew there were dangers in the woods and even from the men employed by the local lord. She brewed a drink from the bark of a yew and implored Woden to send the girl back safely. She held the stone amulet hanging around her neck tightly.

Mark could feel something on his neck. His back ached and his wrist throbbed. He opened his eyes and immediately closed them again as a bright light enveloped him. He realised that the touch on his neck was someone checking for a pulse.

"Thank God you're alive," said a voice. Mark's eyes were getting used to the light and saw it was from the headlights of a Mini and a young lady was standing over him. She was dressed in jeans and a white t-shirt and a pair of lime green trainers. She looked about thirty and she was quite pretty with long blond hair tied loosely at the back. "How do you feel?"

"Like I've been hit by a tractor but I don't think I was. I remember running and jumping over the gate and then … nothing until now."

Mark winced as he sat up gingerly.

"You've got a nasty gash on your arm. I can take you to hospital. By the way, I'm Jade."

"That's very nice of you Jade, my name's Mark. I don't want to put you out so instead of the hospital can you drop me off at my parent's house? It's just down the road a short way."

"Of course I can," she smiled.

Jade helped Mark slowly to his feet and supported him as they made their way to the car. She seated him in the passenger seat and Mark groaned.

It didn't take long for Jade to make a three point turn in the narrow lane and drive the half mile back to the house. Jack must have seen the lights as Jade steered into the driveway and was immediately at the door. Mark had been gone for three hours and they were all a bit worried. Nat rushed out after him and looked angry when he saw another woman in the driving seat but that faded when she saw the state of Mark as he tried to get out of the passenger side of the Mini.

"Mark! What the hell happened?" she almost screamed. Ellie joined her at the door.

"I had some sort of accident down the road. It's my back. Jade just found me lying there unconscious."

Jack saw the gash on Mark's arm and said, "I'll get my keys and take you to hospital, when was the last time you had a tetanus jab?"

"It's got to be a few years, maybe when I was a teenager," answered Mark.

"Okay, that settles it then, thank you for bringing him back Jade, not many would have stopped these days. You're very kind."

"I know what you mean, I'm a social worker and see less and less care and compassion in the world each year. I'm amazed half the country isn't feral by now, but I suppose part of my job is to prevent that."

"Well thanks again Jade, I'd better get Mark to hospital, there's bound to be a long wait in A&E."

"No problem, glad to have helped," Jade smiled. She got back in the Mini and reversed out of the drive back into the lane and drove off waving.

"Nice girl," said Jack. "Let's get you seen to at the hospital."

Jack said to the ladies that there wasn't any point in all of them going and cluttering up the waiting area at A&E and he would call as soon as there was any news. They reluctantly agreed. Ellie had gone back in and found a clean towel in the kitchen and gently wrapped Mark's arm in it. The gash had stopped bleeding while Mark was unconscious but it was the risk of infection Ellie was worried about. Jack helped Mark into the passenger seat and snapped the seat belt into place and moved round to the driver's side of the Mercedes and got in.

"Any idea how you got in this state, Mark?"

"It's all a bit hazy still," he replied. "I remember stopping off at the dell and recalling the times I spent there with my mates and that's about it."

"Is that old car still down there?"

"Yeah, still there, I think it will be there forever. I remember running but don't know why."

"You know you can't run anymore, why the hell would you risk your back by running?"

"I have no idea Dad. It's pretty much all a blank at the moment."

They arrived at the hospital and Jack dropped Mark off at the entrance to the A&E unit and went off to park and then walked back. Mark was already at the reception desk and was explaining what had happened as well as he could recall. The receptionist asked them to take a seat and said he'd be seen as soon as possible. The waiting area was full but they managed to find two seats next to each other at the back of the large room. Most people there just sat silently or dozing off but there was a couple of screaming kids and a drunk with a cut to the head asking every passing nurse when he would be seen as he had some important business to attend to. The important business was probably ordering his next pint. As people were seen their places were filled by new attendees and as the night wore on the kids were replaced by more drunks. Finally after about four hours Mark's name was called and he gingerly walked to a cubicle supported by Jack.

"I'm Doctor Sharma and this is Nurse Jude. Sorry about the wait, we bumped you up the waiting list because you said there was some memory loss so therefore a possibility of a head injury, how are you feeling now?" said the Asian doctor as he checked Mark's scalp for cuts and bumps and found nothing serious.

"My memory is still a bit patchy, I may have hit my head when I blacked out but the main things are my arm and my back. I think the barbed wire I ripped my arm on was rusty and I have a torn disc in my back from a car accident a few years ago."

"I see," said the doctor. "First things first, Nurse Jude will clean the wound on your arm and I'll arrange for an x-ray on your back. I assume you've had an MRI on your back in the past to confirm the disc was torn and not just slipped?"

"Yes, both an x-ray and an MRI a week later, both in this hospital. I was offered an operation eventually but was told that there was a chance of paralysis so opted for pain and slightly limited mobility rather than the chance of being stuck in a wheelchair for life," said Mark.

"I'll check the previous scans just to make sure there is no extra damage. At the moment I'm leaning towards a strain but won't rule anything out as yet."

"Thanks, you are probably right about the strain. I was running but don't know why, I should know better by now."

While the doctor was away Nurse Jude washed out the cut and sutured it and then gave him the anti-tetanus shot. She was an oriental looking lady, maybe Korean or Chinese and possibly about aged about fifty. She had very cold hands even with the latex gloves on.

"I didn't know nurses were allowed to do all that stuff," said Mark.

"Most can't but I'm a Nurse Practitioner, we try and take the strain and do the relatively minor stuff so the doctors can deal with the real life-saving work. There are usually one or two like me in most GP practices now and a lot in A&E."

"It's a great idea, stops the GP's and the emergency docs having to deal with the mundane things like cuts and scrapes and the odd verruca. The paperwork they have to deal with for all that stuff must be horrendous."

"It is, we have to document everything. It's even worse now than when I started nursing thirty years ago."

"It's nice to know I'm in good hands."
Jude smiled and told him it was nice to be appreciated.

Doctor Sharma returned just as Nurse Jude was typing up some notes on the PC at the far end of the cubicle. He was smiling so that gave Mark a bit of relief.

"I see Jude has finished with you so we can get you down to x-ray right away."

He handed Jack a green form.

Mark thanked the doctor and was just about to make his way to the x-ray department when a shaven headed man arrived with a lightweight wheelchair. The man pointed to the small, dark green canvas seat and said, "Please."

"Pavel will take you down and the technician will get your x-ray done and then I'll see you back here in a while," smiled the doctor warmly.

Pavel pushed Mark the short distance to the x-ray department and inside another cubicle Jack helped him out of his clothing and into a wrinkled, white hospital gown. A door next to the cubicle buzzed and a short, balding man of around forty in white wearing thick glasses stuck his head in.

"My name's Ron and I'll be getting your x-ray done in just a minute. I'll just take the form from you while you get yourself laid out on the table."

Jack handed the paper to Ron and then helped Mark lie face down on the cold plastic bench. Ron returned and made sure Mark was positioned correctly and then swung the giant scanner over Mark's hip area. Ron asked Jack to follow him behind the screen and then pressed a large red button and there was a short buzzing sound like an angry wasp in a jam jar.

Mark and Jack moved back into the cubicle and Mark dressed again and outside Pavel was waiting for them with the wheelchair. Mark was wheeled back to the waiting area of A&E and less than 10 minutes later Doctor Sharma came out and told them that there was no additional damage to his back and it should gradually get better over the next few days. He'd also brought out a couple of small white pills for the pain and a cup of water and Mark swallowed both. The doctor also said that his memory should return fairly quickly, there was no apparent head injury but if things didn't improve in a week or he suffered a lot of nausea he needed to see his GP to check him out and maybe a scan was in order but he could see no need for that at the moment. He was confident Mark would remember what happened in a few days. Mark thanked the doctor again and Jack told him to wait by the double doors and he'd go and get the car.

By the time Jack returned the pills were starting to take effect and Mark got into the passenger seat without any need for help.

"That's certainly a relief about your back, it took months for you to recover after the crash. I can't imagine what it's like to lose a portion of your memory though, it must be a little scary."

"It feels like one of those old horror films where the hero loses his memory and thinks he's done something awful but can't remember… and then it turns out that he did."

"Well if we hear about any dead prostitutes in the area in the next few days we'll know where to come," joked Jack.

Mark laughed and said, "It's just so bloody annoying, it's like the thoughts are almost there, nearly grasped and then fade again. Maybe I just need a good night's sleep. Can you do me a favour and call work in the morning and explain what's happened and say I'll be back Tuesday and I'll have a lie in. These pills are making me a bit drowsy already."

"No problem, I can drop Nat off at work too so you can have a good rest."

"Thanks… for everything, dad," he smiled wearily.

They arrived back at the house at a little after one and were met in the driveway by Ellie and Nat who made a fuss of him and got him upstairs to bed. Nat was already in her pajamas and slipped under the duvet beside him and stroked his head, making sure he was comfortable. She asked him what happened but Mark just said he couldn't recall anything at the moment but hopefully it would all come back. It was a complete mystery. He soon fell asleep thanks to the pills the doctor gave him and Nat stayed awake and watched him for about an hour before finally dropping off herself.

Monday April 27th

Mark forced himself awake the next morning near noon. His arm throbbed but his back seemed a little better. He rose and showered trying to keep the dressing on his arm dry and almost succeeded. He dressed slowly and carefully so as not to aggravate his back again and dry swallowed two ibuprofen then trudged downstairs to where Nat and Ellie were in the kitchen baking. The smell of fresh granary bread enveloped the room. They really did love each other's company Mark thought. He could see Jack pottering around in the garden through the kitchen window. Nat told him to sit and after asking how he was feeling started to make him a coffee. Ellie kissed the top of his head and called him 'her little soldier' which made them all laugh. The coffee was strong and black which was how he liked it. Nat was already well trained he thought to himself, she should stick around.

"I thought you were going to work today?" Mark asked.

"I really couldn't be bothered to go in and get leered at all day. Truthfully I don't want to go back at all. You need my attention today. Any luck with the memory?" she asked.

"No, not much. Sometimes I think it's coming and then it pops it's head back in again like a tortoise."

"It'll come, sooner or later."

"I hope it's sooner, it's just so bloody frustrating."

Ellie made more coffee for them all and suggested sitting in the garden for a while. The sun was out but the gentle breeze took away most of the heat. Jack was picking up a few twigs that had dropped from his trees overnight. He assumed it was squirrels jumping from branch to branch at dawn. He came over for a break and sat with them, the heat from his mug of coffee warming his slightly arthritic right hand. Years of pencil pushing he put it down to. Using a pen to manually keep up ledgers before the advent of computers and accounting software. It was just so much easier and quicker today. They chatted for a while about current events. The British PM and the American President seemed to be getting along like best mates which really annoyed the media, another Royal embarrassment was being swept under the carpet and yet another pointless celebrity launched a new book and they joked about who had helped her with the words that were more than four letters long.

"I spoke to Kim earlier babe, she'd like us to go round a bit later to help with things," said Nat.

"Yes, that's fine. I've been feeling a little guilty about shooting off for a break when she needed her friends and family."

"She only got back Saturday so it's not a problem. The boys are staying with their gran until the funeral, so she's alone until then."

"We can nip over after lunch."

"Lunch is just some freshly baked bread and a selection of cheese and pate I'm afraid," piped up Ellie.

"Sounds lovely mum, I'm not really in the mood for something too filling anyway."

"Just eat what you can love, you had a rough end to the day yesterday. Did you sleep alright?"

"Went out like a light as soon as I was tucked up. Those pills the doc gave me really did the trick. Got a good ten hours I suppose. Shame he didn't give me a few extra."

"I wish mine was better, I had a weird dream last night," said Ellie. "It was about a group of people searching the woods for something. It wasn't modern times, maybe a thousand or so years ago by the way they were dressed. Mainly men in long beards and they were frantic. They searched and they searched, one even climbed a huge tree to get a view of the woods. Eventually they found a young girl. She had been torn to pieces by an animal and left at the bottom of a dell but they blamed someone else for it. That's all I remember."

"Strange. No dreams for me as far as I know. That reminds me. I'm supposed to be ringing that artist today."

He took his phone from his pocket and pulled out the number Jim had written an a piece of paper and dialled. It took maybe twenty rings before someone picked up."

"Hello? Brand here, what's your pleasure?"

"Hi, Mr. Brand, my name is Mark Mason and a friend got your number from your website, I hope I'm not bothering you. I don't know what time is best to call an artist. I don't suppose it's like you have a nine to five job."

"You're right. I know some artists work within regular hours but most create when the inspiration hits them. It's mostly in the early hours when I paint. So what can I do for you? I assume it's not to buy one of my paintings or you would have done that on the website."

"No, it's a question about a particular work of yours that I saw in a gallery near Salisbury - it's called Retribution. I wondered what was the inspiration behind it."

"Ah yes. Not my finest but maybe the most memorable for me . Quite simple really. I had a dream about a witch being burnt to death but it wasn't one of those sixteenth century ones like you see in Hammer films or Italian horrors, she was much earlier than that. Maybe a few hundred years before the Puritan witch hunts. In my dream she was accused of a crime of which she was innocent but there were no fancy lawyers or appeals in those days. Most people accused of anything in those days were found guilty one way or another so she never stood a chance. Ended up being burnt in a field tied to a stake."

"So the title refers to the retribution she faced even though she was wrongly accused?"

"No, Mr. Mason - it was for the retribution she would inflict."

Later that afternoon they thought it was time to visit Kim and help out with the funeral arrangements.

"Do you want me to drive?" asked Nat.

"Nice try," he laughed, "I'll be fine."

He started the Jag and chose a Black Sabbath album for the ride over to Kim's house, reluctantly remembering it was not 'Steve and Kim's' anymore. *Paranoid* followed *Never Say Die* which was appropriate as he was feeling a bit wary because of the sequence of events over the last week or so, too many bad things had happened starting with Steve's accident and the latest being his own yesterday afternoon. He'd taken more ibuprofen before they left and his arm didn't feel too bad at the moment but his back felt stiff. Driving wouldn't help, even if he let Nat drive the Beast and he was in the passenger seat, so decided to drive himself. He never thought of himself as a control freak but when it came to his car he was a bit possessive.

It didn't take long for them to pull up in front of Kim's house. They walked to the front door and rang the bell and Kim answered the door wearing bright pink pajamas, her eyes red from crying it seemed. Both of them hugged her and said how sorry they were and were always on the end of a phone if she needed either of them. They sat in the front room and Nat made coffee for them all. She returned with the mugs on a tray and a small plate of biscuits she'd found and they made small talk before Kim got to the important stuff. She had already made the arrangements for the obituary to appear in the local paper at the end of the week but needed help with choosing a funeral director, flowers and the ceremony at the crematorium. She asked Nat to take care of the flowers for her and Mark to visit the funeral director with her and then they could arrange the crematorium for hopefully the following Monday. Steve's remains were still at the hospital morgue and Mark thought how close they were to each other last night when he was being treated. Steve was just one floor below when Mark was having his x-ray.

Mark dropped Nat off at the florist to arrange for the floral tribute provisionally for Monday, which she would hopefully confirm later that day. He and Kim drove to the funeral director, Ashman and Sons in the village, and were attended to by a tall sombre man with short white hair in a morning suit who really did look like everyone's stereotype of an undertaker. Mark thought the expected appearance would put people at ease more - you wouldn't want to talk to someone in a lurid, blue neon suit, it would just be too surreal.

Kim took her time choosing a coffin and had narrowed it down to two when she asked Mark his opinion. He said he liked the mahogany veneer more than the oak one, and suggested the lining was red which was the colour of Steve's football team. Kim agreed so that was the main thing out of the way, then she chose a simple brass urn for the ashes. She told the undertaker that the day had not been finalised but she hoped for Monday. He told her that he could call the crematorium for her right then and arrange that while they waited. She said she'd be very grateful for that. They both found a waiting area away from the display of caskets and sat while Mr. Ashman (such an appropriate name really, thought Mark, although he didn't want to verbalise that for obvious reasons) went to his office to make the call to the crematorium.

Five minutes later he was back and said he had arranged a service for 11 a.m. the following Monday, the coffin would be ready, he'd have the deceased picked up from the morgue and prepare Steve for his final journey. He then asked her how many cars she needed as well as the hearse. She told him just one for immediate family. She appreciated just how painless Mr. Ashman had made things and thanked him. They left and met with Nat as arranged at a pub near the florist. Mark told her that it would be Monday at eleven and she phoned the florist to confirm when she needed the flowers. They sat in a booth and toasted Steve, and Kim thanked the pair of them for all their help. All that was left was to let everyone know about the cremation and then count down the days. Her mum and her sons would arrive on Sunday and she couldn't wait to see the boys again, although it had only been three days since she'd returned from Nottingham. Mark was just about to suggest they move on to the Italian a few doors down from the pub when his phone rang.

"Afternoon, Mr. Mason, it's DI Daly, how were your few days away?"

"Good for the most part, I assume you have some news about the break-in?"

"Yes … and no, we checked the estate agents and found no evidence of any wrongdoing at their end, in fact, apart from the mess in the flat and the note we can't see any evidence at all that there was a break-in."

"Are you saying we made the whole thing up? I can assure you we didn't." He was close to losing his temper.

"No, but I can only act on evidence and as I said there is none. All I'm prepared to say is I've come across some strange things over the years. Things that just don't make sense if you look at things logically, but they are things that just can't take up police resources, I'm sorry. I believe something happened, but officially it has to remain unsolved."

"I can't say I'm not disappointed, but I can see it from your perspective, thanks anyway, Inspector."

Mark hung up and explained to Nat what the call was about. He had to check for available flats online later and get something arranged, he also needed to cancel the tenancy and find somewhere else, he just couldn't go back to that flat and spend the night. Paying to end the agreement and the deposit for another place would be expensive and he'd probably have to pay for a other month's rental but it would be worth it in the long run. He'd make sure the new place was alarmed and had security cameras outside too. Maybe if he'd had that at the old place the police would have more to go on and even footage of the burglars breaking in although they technically weren't burglars in the eyes of the police if they didn't attempt to steal anything. Mark was still convinced they had the wrong flat.

They eventually did get to the Italian and ordered traditional pasta meals and sat and talked about everything and anything except the funeral. Mark couldn't imagine the shock Kim had gone through when she discovered Steve on top of the lawn mower and never wanted to. Suddenly his salsa di pomodoro wasn't so appealing.

They finished their meal and Mark drove Kim home, asking if she wanted them to stay for a while. Kim said she was alright and had to make a start on contacting people about the funeral and the sooner she got that done the better and she could relax a little. Nat told her to call for any reason at all and they would be there for her. She thanked them yet again, said goodnight and hugged them both.

Mark needed something soothing and mellow on the stereo for the trip back and hit 4 on the CD changer and the smooth sounds of Robin Trower eased out through the speakers. He was also one of Nat's favourites too and by the time they got back to their temporary home they felt a lot more relaxed. They walked in while Jack and Ellie where still eating and told them about their afternoon and the arrangements made. They sat at the dining table while the others finished their meal and then Jack poured drinks for them. White wine for Ellie and Nat while Jack drained the last of the ten year old single malt for himself and Mark. They drank to Steve and wished Kim all the best.

Mark and Nat decided they had to look at flats.They searched the sites of three local letting agents and Mark thought it would be easier to buy but he didn't want to get tied down with a mortgage on his wages and even if

Nat moved in it would stretch them financially. They were stuck with renting and properties in their area were way overpriced but it was either that or go back to the old flat and neither wanted to do that, not without some major security upgrades provided by the landlord but there was no way he would pay for that. There was really just one option, a flat above the greengrocer in Marsham village. One bedroom, bathroom, kitchen and lounge. There was just one entrance, it was at the rear of the shop and there was parking in the courtyard there. The flat was alarmed and there was CCTV covering the courtyard. Everything looked good apart from the rent which was nearly one thousand per month, furnished. Mark said he'd call the agents tomorrow lunchtime. He'd have to go back to work in the morning.

The party searching for Wilda finally found her. She was wedged between two trees at the bottom of a deep depression in the woods … or what was left of her was. There were deep gashes all over her partially naked body and some of her fingers were missing. Her hair, streaked with blood, hung over her face. Her father, Ware, wailed in emotional agony. His friend Alwin placed a hand on his shoulder and bowed his head.

"I'm sorry, my friend. She must have been attacked by wolves on her way home."

"NO! It was the witch!"

"But why would she? She liked the girl and was tutoring her in the ways of a healer. It doesn't make sense, Ware."

"Look at her! She was sacrificed! Something only a witch would do."

"Come, let's wrap her and take her home where she can be prepared."

There was a murmuring amongst the rest of the men while Ware and Alwin wrapped Wilda's body in Ware's cloak. Ware's rage at the witch had put seeds of doubt in their minds. If he was right there would be serious consequences not only for Mother Watkin but for the rest of them too.

Ware trudged through the woods with Wilda in his arms, tears streaming down his face. Partly in sorrow but also with rage at the witch. It was her! He was convinced. The rest of the men followed in silence, beginning to be equally convinced in their own minds. Watkin must pay for this!

Tuesday April 28th

The next morning Mark and Nat both rose at seven. Mark wanted to go to his flat and change into his work clothes and to pick up a couple more shirts to keep at his parent's house. He also needed to clear out the fridge so would come back after work and do that. They left the flat and Mark dropped Nat off in front of the jeweller and he sped off in the Jag for the commercial area of town. He parked and bought a coffee from the kiosk in the car park as usual and took the lift to the third floor then walked down the corridor to his office. John, the effeminate manager, was there talking to someone Mark had never seen before, a tall, spindly youth of about eighteen or nineteen with red hair and a face covered in freckles. He was wearing a three piece suit and Mark thought he was maybe from head office.

"Mark, good to see you. How are you feeling? This is James. He joined us yesterday and is pretty much up to speed already but if he needs any help can you oblige? I was on the phones most of last week and have quite a bit to catch up with in my office."

Mark shook hands with James and said it wasn't a problem. James had a grip like a cold fish. Mark chatted a little with him before it was time to get on the phones and start conning unsuspecting customers.

The morning went quite quickly, James only asked for help once which was good. He seemed a lot more with it than Paul had been when he had started. Lunch time came and Mark gave the letting agent a call and arranged to view at around six after he'd picked Nat up from work. James had left the building and ventured out to the nearest fast food place which would be full of people his own age at this time of day. Mark wasn't that hungry so went down to the kiosk and queued for about ten minutes to get a sausage roll and a cup of coffee. They would see him through until the evening when he planned to take Nat to the pub in Marsham for a meal. Hopefully they'd be celebrating.

By the end of the work day he'd had more than enough and rushed out to meet Nat. He was feeling hopeful as he jumped into the Jag and Judas Priest's *Breaking the Law* announced itself from the stereo. He wasn't a big fan but they had produced half a dozen great tunes over the years. Mark parked a few car lengths down from the front of the jewellers and it didn't take Nat long to spot him. She eased herself into the passenger seat and buckled up and was grinning to herself.

"What's so funny?" asked Mark.

"Just excited, I wasn't with you when you rented the old place and I've never viewed before."

"Hopefully it will be good enough, I just don't want any more disappointments at the moment. We have a new guy at work, James, he seems alright. At least he doesn't seem to be a Billy Big Balls like Paul was. Didn't talk about himself too much which is a good sign."

They arrived at Marsham high street a little before six and the agent was there waiting for them. The man struggled out of his red Micra and Mark thought he was the spitting image of the old actor Sydney Greenstreet from Bogart classics like *Casablanca* and *The Maltese Falcon.* The only thing missing was the white suit wrapping his rotund frame.

"You must be Mark," he said. "My name is Sydney." Mark almost laughed out loud. He expected to meet a bulging eyed Peter Lorre hiding in the flat to complete the ridiculous scenario.

"Hi, yes and this is Natalie."

"Pleased to meet you, young lady," he said rolling out the charm of a born salesman. "The flat hasn't been on the market long. The last tenant left a couple of months ago and the landlord took the opportunity to refurbish. New paper, paint and upgraded the plumbing too. Also a lot of new furniture, I'm sure he has shares in IKEA," he chuckled.

They moved towards an alley at the side of the greengrocer, the shop was empty apart from a woman in overalls sweeping the floor, she looked up as they passed and then lost interest. Mark wondered what sort of smells greeted the occupants of the flat upstairs every morning. They got to the courtyard behind the shop and Mark noticed the CCTV cameras, three in all, that would deter any intruder. That was already a big plus point. There was a narrow black iron staircase leading up to a balcony. It looked to have been freshly painted, no rust at all. Sydney led the way up the stairs, his weight making each step groan as he ascended. Mark thought if it could take Sydney's weight it was good for a few years yet and at least he didn't get stuck halfway. Nat followed him up and Mark brought up the rear. From the balcony Sydney turned and said to them:

"Obviously the view from the windows at the front are pretty ordinary, just your usual village high street but at the back you can see a fair bit of countryside and beyond those woods are Marsham Stones, are you familiar with them?"

"Yes, we've visited them quite a lot, we love the area," said Mark.

"I don't live too locally but I sometimes visit with my little dog, he is fine walking around the outside of the stones but he won't enter the circle for some reason. Maybe it's something animals can pick up and we can't. One of those little mysteries that keeps life interesting I suppose."

He fished a key out of his jacket pocket and opened the front door. Sydney prodded a four digit code into a panel to his left and they entered. There was still the faint odour of fresh paint in the air. That would soon dissipate with the widows left open for a few hours. There was a short corridor pointing towards a front room overlooking the street and to the left there was a good sized kitchen, a large sink beneath a window looking out to the rear, a gas cooker, plenty of cupboards and counters and a giant fridge/freezer, plenty of electric sockets for toaster, kettle and other gadgets too. There was a pine table in the centre with a lot of room all around on cream floor tiles. The kitchen looked very clean and Mark could see from Nat's face she was impressed. He was too, it was a good start.

Opposite the kitchen was a good sized bathroom, there was a large bath and also a small shower in the corner. There was also a double sink with a mirror above each so that two people could get ready in the mornings without fighting over space, and a toilet in between the bath and sinks underneath a frosted rectangular window about a yard across. It was the biggest bathroom Mark had ever seen. Everything was lime green which he liked. Much better that the bog standard brilliant white. He laughed to himself at the pun. He even liked the floor which was a Victorian design of triangular shapes in white, black and a paler green.

Next to the bathroom was a small airing cupboard with plenty of shelving for towels and spare bedding and then they came to the bedroom. A huge double bed was centred along one wall, there was a 'his and hers' set of wardrobes on either side of the bed and also a hanging rail for clothes and a shoe rack underneath. Nat gasped at the large dressing table with a mirror situated under the window. There was a big TV that looked to be at least twenty-four inches mounted on the wall and a DVD player on a shelf underneath. The walls were a deep, warm red, almost burgundy, the colour of a velvet cloak with a carpet to match on the floor and a shaggy white rug at the foot of the bed.

The L-shaped living room was quite spacious with a two and a three seater pair of leather sofas around a glass topped table, a giant forty inch LCD TV with a DVD player and a stacked retro style stereo system on a table next to it. At the far end of the room was a dining table that would comfortably seat six with padded chairs arranged around it. The walls were papered and had a Chinese design which Mark loved. The carpet was beige and Mark thought that was the only drab feature in the entire flat. Sydney was right, the view from the massive picture window was nothing to write home about but there was a lot of light coming into the room even at this time of a spring evening.

"I can tell you're impressed," beamed Sydney. I wouldn't mind living here myself except the landlord doesn't want pets, you don't have any do you?"

"Only my boss," joked Mark. "Neither of us smoke either … anything."

"So I assume you are interested. I'm not sure how long this place will be available but if you decide to take it I can get everything arranged by the end of the week including a credit check and reference. There is also a month's deposit and subsequent payments are in advance by standing order."

"They won't be a problem. The reference you could probably get is from my current landlord through Whittaker's who I lease from. My credit check should be fine, I never miss a credit card payment and rarely go into my overdraft. My credit score must be pretty good."

"Excellent," said Sydney. "I'll let you both talk it over tonight and if you can give me a ring in the morning it will be much appreciated. Would this be a joint tenancy? If so I'd need two references and a credit check on each of you."

"To be honest, we're not sure yet, something else to decide this evening."

Nat took Mark's hand and gave it a squeeze.

"I quite understand, it's a big step for you young people."

"Thank you for showing us around, I'll definitely give you a call in the morning and let you know."

They said good evening as Sydney squeezed back in the Micra, waved and left, they turned and walked hand in hand to the pub fifty yards down the high street.

The Peacock was starting to get busy but they found a table in the corner and Mark ordered steak and chips at the bar and a pint for himself and a cheese salad with white wine for Nat.

"It's really lovely," said Nat.

"Yes, it's really nice, bit expensive for one, maybe not for two," smiled Mark.

"You want me to move in too?"

"You stay with me three or four nights a week anyway, it wouldn't be much different and I doubt I could afford it for more than a few months on my own."

"I'd love to Mark, if all goes well we could move in at the weekend."

"What about a reference for you? All I can think of is your boss and he seems to have a crush on you. Probably wouldn't be happy about you moving in with me."

"I was thinking about that, I was reading up on tenant references last night and it seems that someone can act as a guarantor instead, and I was thinking....."

"My dad! He's certainly someone 'in good standing' and has the cash and would probably love to. He thinks a lot of you, you know."

"I love both your parents too, they have really made me feel welcome. I love my mum but she really doesn't show much affection towards me, or anyone else for that matter. She still feels bitter about my dad leaving and that was twenty odd years ago. And I haven't had any contact from my dad in over a year. Last I heard he was still on the rigs. Your mum and dad are like surrogate parents to me."

"I have Sydney's mobile number, should I ring him now or wait until the morning?" Mark grinned.

"Leave it until tomorrow, he's probably relaxing or taking his dog for a walk by now. I really want to get back and tell your parents before anyone else."

"Can we wait until after my steak? I'm bloody starving!"

The meals arrived and were very good but they both rushed, eager to get back with the news. On the way back Mark took the lane near the dell he'd visited two days before. He still couldn't remember anything except running over the field and then waking up with Jade leaning over him checking for a pulse. Did something scare him? What the hell was it? The ride back didn't take much longer and Mark told his parents the news that he was going to take the flat they had viewed and Nat would be moving in with him.

Marks parents acted like it was an engagement announcement and Jack dug out a bottle of champagne from his drinks cabinet. Mark felt a little embarrassed but let them have their moment. Jack said he'd rent a van and help Mark move what little there was of his own things from the old flat.

"Looks like the golf day is off with your dodgy arm so we may as well spend the time getting you settled in. They won't take long to get you both approved so I can I see it being Saturday or Sunday at the latest before we get rid of you both," he laughed. "I like Marsham and you are only a few yards from a decent pub and it would be a bit safer than the old place. I had a look online today and it's certainly an upgrade on the old flat."

"I think we both fell in love with it as soon as we got through the door," said Mark. "Nat was positively drooling over the kitchen."

"Sexist pig!" she joked as she gave him a playful dig in the ribs with her elbow. "You'll be doing your fair share of cooking too."

Nat called her mum and gave her the news but the reaction wasn't as happy as the one from Mark's parents. Her mum practically said that Nat was abandoning her like her dad did all those years ago and that upset Nat. She tried to explain that she would have had to leave eventually and live her own life and not end up as an old maid. She did understand that her mum would feel lonely but she told her that she needed to get out more and make friends, go to the bingo or organised day trips somewhere on a coach. She had to do something, start to enjoy herself. The call ended with her mum saying she'd think about it. Nat looked a little down and Ellie, who had heard one side of the conversation and guessed the other half, gave Nat a hug.

They came for Mother Watkin the next day. Men who served Lord Machen the Thane of the village. A Thane governed a village or area on behalf of the King. They were armed with spears and axes and pulled her roughly from her small hut.

"I have done nothing!" screamed Watkin.

"The girl was found, she was mutilated. Sacrificed. By you, says her father. He has accused you of dark magic. You have to come with us," said one of the men holding her tightly by the wrist. Another uncoiled some hemp rope and tied her hands behind her back."

"I am innocent!" she cried. "You will regret this Oswald Adney!"

"I feel you will regret this more," sneered the stocky man with a huge black beard.

They marched her through the woods for almost four miles. The Thane's manor house was extensive and made from wood and had a thatched roof. There was also a great hall used to entertain the Lord and his guests. Scattered around were also various huts for servants and a stable. Behind the stable was a pit which was covered in a rough mesh of twigs. Watkin was dragged to the pit, her binding cut from her hands and she was thrown into the dank shaft and the cover lowered again and pinned by two large boulders.

"My Lord will deal with you at his leisure, pray he takes his time, witch!"

With the cover lowered the pit was in almost total darkness. She sat on the mud at the bottom and implored Woden to save her. She knew she was innocent of any crime and so would he. Watkin was sorry about the girl but she had no part in her death. Even with no proof the Lord had power over life and death and she doubted she'd survive. She knew that to be accused of witchcraft almost certainly meant she would be executed. She had to use the dark magic of which she was accused, after all. There was no point in protesting her innocence anymore. The stone amulet around her neck could be used to preserve her spirit. She was told this by her grandmother who was a powerful witch in her own right. Her grandmother had taught her certain incantations and made her swear that she would only use them as a last resort - when all else had failed. The stone around her neck had been chipped from one of the giant granite blocks that formed a stone circle nearby. They were from another time and had immense power. On one side were runes and on the reverse was a portrait of a demon. It was to Anrok she now prayed to. She formed a spell and heat emanated from the stone. She welcomed the warmth in the cold pit.

Wednesday April 29th

Mark called Sydney next morning from work and got the ball rolling.

Sydney took down their employment details and also their bank information and said it should only take a couple of days, maybe three. Mark also called his current letting agency and told them he would not be prepared to continue with the tenancy after the break-in and would return the keys after he'd picked up his belongings. They tried to talk him out of it but soon found that he was adamant. They informed him that he'd need to pay the rent up to the end of the next month and his deposit would be returned minus any damages and after they had sent a cleaner into the property. He was fairly happy with that. It was best to cut his losses with that place. Mark was getting quite excited about moving into the new flat. The check would be a formality even if Nat's boss decided to be difficult over his petty jealousy. There was always his dad able to be a guarantor if he needed to be.

The rest of the day went pretty quickly. The new lad was doing well and had made a few deals already. Mark had signed up a lot of customers for the dodgy phone contracts too. He was motivated not only because he needed the money after taking almost a whole week off, but because he wanted to make a home with Nat. There! It seemed like he had decided this was a long term thing with her. It had been creeping up on him for a while. Had he given in after a little pressure from his parents and even Steve and Kim or was it something he always wanted? Tucked up in his brain like a chrysalis finally hatching into a butterfly. He was in a pretty good mood as he finished for the day and went to pick Nat up from work.

He was there in plenty of time and as he waited he remembered that he had to get to the old flat to clear out the fridge and freezer . They could take the frozen food back with them and bin the rest. Everything in the fridge would have to go, especially the milk as well as a few slices of ham that had been in there for at least a week. He was sure the eight cans of Stella and a half bottle of vodka would be fine though and thought he would have a couple of cans tonight.

Nat came out of the jewellers with a big smile. She told him that her boss had a call from the letting agents and given her good reference. Mark looked at her in shock and then he smiled too. Things were looking up for them after a bad couple of weeks. They both felt they appreciated the good things more instead of taking them for granted.

The trip back to the flat didn't take too long. He'd nipped in to the local supermarket on the way and got a big yellow insulated bag to hold the frozen food and the drinks. The rest was just thrown into a black plastic bin bag and dumped in the communal bin at the back of the flats. Mark also grabbed his laptop and earbuds. The rest could wait until they moved. Hopefully at the weekend.

On the trip back to Mark's parent's Nat's ringtone burst into life. Mark turned down the stereo from the control on the steering wheel and Joe Cocker faded into the background. Nat frowned when she saw her mum's name come upon the smartphone's screen. She really wanted to avoid another guilt trip.

"Hi mum," she said.

"Natalie, I've just had a call from the police and thought you should know. Your dad has gone missing in Aberdeen. He hasn't been seen for about a week. They called me because he has me listed as next of kin for some reason. He's probably on a bender and shacked up with some old tart," she said vindictively.

"Oh my God! I hope he's alright. I really hope they find him soon, I know you don't care about him but I do, he's still my dad."

"I know that Natalie. Maybe if he turns up you can ask him to change his next of kin to you. You know I washed my hands of him a long time ago."

Nat didn't want an argument after what, up until then, had been a good day. "Okay mum, I hope I get the chance to do that. I have to go now, bye."

"What happened?" asked Mark.

"My dad is missing in Aberdeen, no one has seen him for a week. The police called my mum to inform her."

"Bloody hell, that's a worry. I hope he surfaces. I haven't even met him yet."

"I'll phone my mum again later and see if she knows who I can contact up there. Even if she doesn't care I'd like to be the one they call with any updates."

That night Ellie had another dream. A woman was being dragged through the woods by a group of men and then dumped in a big hole and the entrance was blocked. She heard the babble of voices that had gathered near the opening but could only decipher the odd word in the cacophony of sound. She could feel the hopelessness and despair the woman had for her mortal body. The hole was about ten feet deep and almost pitch black, she sat on damp mud at the bottom of the shaft and rotting vegetables lay all around her. The smell was awful and she tried not to gag. The woman knew that if she was in there any length of time she would have to eat the putrid food. She knew she would die. Was it better to starve than the way planned for her? She doubted she'd be given the time to starve anyway. She was accused of a great crime but she was innocent. No amount of pleading would save her. There was only one way to keep her spirit alive.

Ellie woke from the dream in the early hours of the morning. She tossed and turned for a while and decided to get up for a short spell so that she didn't wake Jack. She padded to the bedroom door and slipped through, closing it quietly and made her way down the carpeted stairs to the kitchen. She turned on the lights and filled the kettle and turned it on. She chose her favourite mug, one with Pooh Bear and Piglet on it that Mark had bought her as a birthday present when he was seven or eight, and reached into the cupboard above the kettle and chose one of her fruit teas, a nice strawberry and elderflower. Kettle boiled, she filled her mug and let the brew infuse for a few minutes before taking the bag out. She sat at the kitchen table and wondered why her dreams had become so vivid recently. They all seemed connected somehow. Strangely the dreams hadn't faded like normal ones. She still remembered large fragments of the ones over the last couple of weeks. That was so unusual for her. Dreams usually disappeared from her mind as soon as she woke like a leaf that had been blown into a river and receding into the distance on the current. Maybe it was another symptom of the menopause? There seemed to be so many. She sighed out loud and took her first sip of tea, wincing slightly as the hot liquid touched her lips. She blew on the contents of the mug and set it on the table to cool a little. It was then she noticed the fog outside the large sliding doors of her kitchen. It was so thick she couldn't make out anything in the garden, not even the concrete slabs of the patio. She wondered if the wildlife still scuttled through the fog or did they all hide, tucked up under some leaves or in a bush or climbed a tree. Were they scared of the fog or was it just another part of nature they were used to?

She vaguely saw a shape drifting through the heavy vapour. Was it her imagination or was something roaming around the garden? She thought it was the cherry tree in the centre of the lawn but it appeared to be moving from left to right. I must be a trick of the light. The moon endeavouring to cut it's way through the fog, trying to bring comfort and normality to those like her who could not sleep or those who worked night shifts in factories and warehouses. She got up and moved closer to the glass, straining her eyes to see what was causing the movement. Her hand moved slowly to the white lever that locked the sliding UPVC door. She hesitated, fingers hovering over it ready to lift it up to release the lock. Should she go out and investigate? What if there was a burglar out there? Using the fog as cover and trying to find a way in? If she lived in the wilds of America it could have been a bear, one unlike Pooh though. Maybe even a Bigfoot. She laughed at herself inwardly at how ridiculous that was. She supposed it could have been a deer that had squeezed through the bushes that separated the garden from the fields at the far end, a Muntjac maybe. She knew there were a few in the area, supposedly escaped from Whipsnade Zoo nearby like the colony of wallabies that have been roaming the woods and fields of Hertfordshire and Bedfordshire for the last fifty or sixty years. She'd never seen a wallaby in the wild but she had seen the odd Muntjac in the woods bordering the road up to the chalk hills of Ivinghoe Beacon. She'd even seen a Roe on one of her walks in the local countryside. She'd noticed it sticking it's head out from from trees, watching her. When she'd stopped walking the deer seemed to assess it's options and then bolted from it's cover and ran down a track away from Ellie and vaulted a barbed wire fence and over a hill. She did however manage to get her phone out in time and took a couple of pictures, one of just the head poking through the trees, and another as it raced towards the barbed wire. She was relieved it wasn't snagged on the fence.

She decided against going outside, discretion being the better part of valour and all that. Her nose was pressed against the glass trying to see if there was any more movement. BANG! There was a thump on the window that made her jump back and she bumped into the table hurting her thigh. Her mug of tea sloshed and spilt hot liquid on the table. What the hell was that? A bird flying towards the light? As far as she knew birds didn't fly in the dead of night. A bat? Suddenly she had no wish to find out. She backed away from the window after checking the lock was in the down and locked position and turned off the light. Her tea forgotten, she left the kitchen and returned to bed and snuggled up to Jack who grunted and carried on snoring. It took a while for her to drift off to sleep, her imagination running riot.

Thursday April 30th

She woke late for her that morning, around eight-fifteen, and took a cold shower. Jack was already up and she assumed he was having breakfast. She quickly dried herself off, dressed and walked slowly downstairs. There was no sign of Jack or the others. Mark and Nat would have left for work so she didn't really expect them to still be there. Her mug from last night was washed and on the counter next to the kettle. She filled the kettle again and went to the sliding door and looked out. Still no sign of Jack. Ellie's hand moved to the door lock lever and saw that it was already in the open position, she slid the door open and walked out onto the patio. She ambled out onto the lawn, the grass cold on the soles of her feet, the odd blade sticking up between her toes and tickling slightly, when she looked in horror at what was six feet in front of her. A patch of blood about two feet square and it looked fresh, the sun was glinting off the slick surface.

Her first thought was Mark's friend Steve and the accident he'd had in his own garden then she thought of Jack. Had he injured himself and wandered off into the bushes and collapsed?

"JACK!" she screamed. Panic started to invade her thoughts. Where was he? "Jack, are you all right? Where are you?"

"I'm here," he said as he exited the path that ran along the side of the house. "Just dealing with the mess."

"The blood … I thought it was yours!"

"No, I found a bird ripped to pieces and got rid of it. Threw it onto the farmland in front of the house."

"There is so much of it."

"Who knew there is that much blood in a crow? I had no idea. Maybe the dew diluted it a bit and it spread. Must have been a cat I suppose, maybe a fox. Anyway, it's pretty much dealt with, I'll get the garden hose out in a minute and wash the blood away and then we can sit down and relax a bit. You're up late. Did you sleep well?"

Ellie thought about telling Jack about her nocturnal interlude last night but decided not to. Was it the bird that had made the noise on the glass? Maybe. She wasn't sure. A big crow that didn't know night from day and had been flying around in the fog suddenly flew into the door as she looked out? Surely she would have seen it and wouldn't there be some evidence on the glass? She could imagine a cat dragging an injured, or even dead, bird out to the centre of the lawn and playing with it before ripping it to pieces though. Probably that big black thing from three houses down. Too fat to catch birds by itself so picked on what it could get.

"I slept on and off, got up for a bit," she said vaguely.

"I saw your mug of tea, looked like you forgot all about it. I washed it and got it ready for breakfast."

"Thanks love."

Ellie went in and made some coffee and toast while Jack washed the blood away. She still felt uneasy about last night, both the incident in the kitchen and the dreams she'd been having. She tried to put it to the back of her mind as she planned her day. She was going to do a bit of gardening but decided to put it off for today. Maybe she'd take a little trip into town and window shop for a while and then stop off at the butcher in Marsham and get something special for later.

Ellie and Jack sat at the table on the patio eating breakfast and making small talk. Her eyes kept returning to the wet patch of grass where the puddle of blood was before Jack had hosed it away. Bloody cats, she thought.

After her meal she called Nat's mum to see if she was alright after her call from the police the day before. Nat's mum seemed even surlier than usual and pretty much intimated she wanted to be left alone. Ellie liked her but felt sorry for her too. Maybe she was hurt by Nat's dad leaving but letting it fester and consume her for the last twenty years was sad and pointless. She could have made another life for herself and not dwell on the hate she had for her ex-husband. According to Nat there wasn't anyone else involved, just the rejection. Ellie told her that if there was anything she needed she was only a phone call or a short ride away and said goodbye. It must have been hard on Nat too but she had tried to put everything behind her and make the best of it, seeing her dad on birthdays and at Christmas would have seemed normal to her although he was never allowed in the house. Her dad would have dialled the land line at the house and waited for three rings and put the phone down and Nat would jump out of the front door and run excitedly to the call box at the end of the street where her dad would be patiently waiting. After Nat had saved enough to buy her own mobile phone there was no need for the three ring announcement that he was at the call box, even in her late teens she ran down the road to his hugs and kisses. She was mature enough to know that her dad hadn't left *her* when he'd walked out all those years ago, it was just grown up stuff. Ellie was suddenly proud of how well Nat had coped with not only having a full time single parent but also a part time one too, a lot of kids have turned out rebellious and even bad in similar circumstances. Ellie smiled and started to fantasise about organising a wedding. She realised she loved Nat like she was one of her own. Hopefully in the next year or two. Give them time to get used to each other in the new flat.

Ellie spent the next couple of hours window shopping but didn't buy

anything. She was very tempted to buy a new summer dress. The weather was good at the moment and the summers seemed to be getting warmer in recent years. Maybe she'd get one on her next visit to town. She stopped off at the jewellers to ask Nat if she wanted to go for lunch, she'd like to have a chat. She wanted to tell Nat of the call she made to Nat's mum and to say she was a bit worried about her. The call about her missing husband had brought out even more hate for him. Maybe she resented the attention he was getting? Nat said she could go to lunch in another thirty minutes so Ellie said she'd wait for her in the pub.
Ellie sat in a corner of the pub with a pint of lemonade as she never drank if she was driving. The pub was nice and cool and she was glad to be relaxing after her dream and the worry about Jack that morning. Nat arrived and Ellie ordered a Ploughman's for each of them and an orange juice for Nat. Nat agreed that her mum was very bitter towards her dad and she had tried for years to get her to go out more and make a new life but her mum just wasn't interested and seemed to enjoy wallowing in self pity. She couldn't think of anything else she could try. She'd even suggested counselling which made her mum even worse and positively hostile. She was close to giving up because her mum just wouldn't change. Hate for her ex-husband was the norm for her now.

Ellie needed to confide in someone about her dreams. She told Nat of the vivid images that came to her at night and how interesting and yet oppressive they were. She felt part of the events, connected to one or more of the characters in the scenes. Nat said that she believed that when we had a dream from the past that it was some sort of memory passed down from an ancestor. That was how events felt so real, they had actually happened to someone far back in the bloodline. Ellie thought that was a very interesting concept. She had thought that her love of history and the fiction she read had influenced her but dreaming of a passed down memory, if possible, made a lot of sense. She had long believed that when someone saw a ghost that they were seeing a recording from the past, called the Stone Tape theory, an event captured in time by some sort of energy embedded in a particular place so why not a memory passed down and stored in her DNA? That somehow calmed her but also concerned her than one of her ancestors could be involved in dragging that poor woman from her home and imprisoning her in that awful pit. Then she had a more disturbing thought... Maybe that woman was her?

After their lunch Ellie walked Nat back to work and told her she was going to make something special for dinner and to make sure Mark didn't take her out for a meal. They hugged and Nat entered the shop to finish her day. Ellie walked to her dark blue Ford and drove to Marsham high street, she bought four pheasant breasts from the butcher and then made her way to the greengrocer just down the road. She looked up at the flat above the shop and looked forward to helping Mark and Nat move in and make a home for themselves. In the shop she picked up some green beans, rocket and a couple of red bell peppers. She'd not cooked pheasant for a while and never with salad. Her mouth was already watering.

As she was already in Marsham she decided to visit the stones. It had been a few years since she'd walked around the circle. She always found the site soothing and she was still a bit uneasy after her panic when she thought the blood on the lawn belonged to Jack. She needed to feel at peace again. She drove to the small grass car park and walked through the copse to the circle and headed for the largest of the eleven monoliths. Putting both hands on the giant stone she could feel the energy it emitted, a slight buzzing that she felt creeping down her arms and into the core of her body. It was like recharging a battery to her. The negativity draining from her into the ground of the stone ring. Had her ancestors ever done the same thing? She had always been attracted to the boulders there and Nat's suggestion it could be some sort of race memory could explain that.

Feeling rejuvenated she decided to get home and make a start on the meal. The sun shone down on her and she could feel the warm rays on her face, all was good now. As she entered the copse the temperature suddenly dropped. There was no sound at all. The birds were silent and the only thing she heard was her stepping on the occasional twig. A blanket of fog was coming towards her, and she'd have to be careful getting back to her car. She didn't worry about getting lost in it but she thought her bumbling through the trees would take her ages and she'd have trouble finding her car. Then she remembered the fog during the night, the fleeting shape in it and feeling that there was something malevolent on the other side of the kitchen door. She looked all around her, now worried she was in danger. Trying not to get disorientated she picked up the pace, making sure she didn't trip over anything by straying off the narrow path. The thick vapour was oppressive as she tried to find her way out of it. She heard more twigs snapping but it wasn't her. It sounded off to her left but it was hard to make out the exact location. She hoped it was a fox or a badger but what if it was something else? She was close to panic now. The other possibilities raced through her mind, maybe it was a man, a serial killer who preyed on women like a modern day Jack the Ripper. It was always foggy when he attacked his victims in Victorian London, wasn't it? She scraped her knuckles on the bark of a tree and winced as it started to sting. Her foot slipped on something and she hoped it was something benign and not a pile of dog mess or even worse the remains of some animal. The fog was getting into her lungs now and she started to cough, wondering what sort of pollution could be in it. As she inched forward she could see a dark shape in front of her. She stopped, dead in her tracks, tried to be as quiet as she could. What was it? It wasn't moving. How could she defend herself if she needed to? She remembered the car key in her pocket. She fumbled it out and gripped the long shaft between her fingers for protection. Then she heard a 'blip' and saw a pair of flashing amber lights. It was her car, she must have pressed the button on the fob and unlocked it. Ellie felt a sense of relief as she carefully made her way to the car, opened the door, and bundled herself into the driver's seat. She sat there, heart racing and hyperventilating, closing her eyes and trying to take deep breaths. She hit the lock on the door and immediately felt a lot safer. She'd wait for the fog to lift a little before she'd attempt to drive home. She turned the key in the ignition and tried the lights but they didn't cut through the gloom to any extent. She hit the button for the stereo and Janis Joplin roared loudly. Ellie turned up the volume and closed her eyes again. A guttural laugh came from the fog but she didn't hear it.

Mother Watkin had already resigned herself to the thought of dying but it would *only be temporary. The power of the amulet around her neck would ensure that. Then she would come back for her revenge. She would conceal the amulet and then when it was found the demon would return and make five sacrifices so that she could become almost whole again, becoming more complete after each death. Then she would make the sixth sacrifice herself. Not only alive but immortal! Her grandmother had once told her the story of the demon Anrok who could grant eternal life. It was Anrok who was carved on the stone and would carry out the first five sacrifices for her.*

They came for her at dawn the next day. A baying mob eager for the execution. There was no trial, no chance to protest her innocence. A man jumped into the pit and lifted her emaciated body so that she could be grabbed and hauled from the pit. Her hands were then tied but no one saw what was concealed in her fist. She was knocked to the ground and two men clutched her ankles with strong hands and she was dragged over the wet, muddy ground for what seemed like miles. She lifted her head and in the distance she could see a stout pole sticking up from the ground. She knew what it was for and she didn't have much time left. She slowly opened her hand and the amulet dropped onto the mud, soon trampled deep by the crowd following the death procession. The horde of shouting villagers were getting louder and more excited as they reached the pole. Watkin was pulled to her feet and tied to the thick oak mast. The villagers had brought bundles of twigs and dried leaves with them and in turn laid them around the pole. The last man to do so was Ware. He bent, put his bundle of kindling at her feet and rose to his full height and spat at her. Oswald

Adney, the Thane's head man moved through the crowd carrying a flaming torch.

"My lord Machen has found you guilty of witchcraft and the sacrifice of Wilda, daughter of Ware. You knew the punishment for using dark magic and so shall you burn and your body disposed of. Such evil will not be tolerated in this or any other village of his land."

"Ware! You know I am innocent. I loved your daughter!" cried Watkin. "I will return to avenge this false charge, and your whole family will suffer!"

Adney passed the torch to Ware who smiled at Watkin and lowered the torch to the kindling. The dry leaves and twigs crackled as they caught light and the fire soon spread all around the pole that Watkin was tied to. Watkin screamed in anger. The rage in her was part of the spell, the amulet would complete it. The scorching flames rose higher. She screamed until the all consuming fire engulfed her and she could scream no more.

Later that day when the fire was out and the white ashes cold, two men took what was left of her charred body and carried it to Devil's Pond, named because it was said to be so deep it reached Hell itself. They weighted her with thick chains and threw her bodily remains into the deep water.

Dominic Brand had just finished his latest work in his studio which was converted from one of the spare bedrooms. The painting wasn't a masterpiece, he thought, but it would sell to a certain following. He stepped back and viewed the painting without any sense of pride. It was just another off the conveyor belt of his imagination or dreams, created to maintain his lifestyle which was fairly comfortable. He wasn't a stereotypical 'starving painter' suffering for their art. He lived in a four bedroom detached house on the outskirts of Salisbury. The house was as remote as you could get, about a mile away from the nearest other property. He was happy with the location, the land around him providing inspiration for the many landscapes he had produced over the years. He was no Turner though. His views of farmland and animals sold but not as well as the darker paintings he'd produced. The ones that came to him in the dreams. The new painting was one of those. The foreground was dominated by a leering demon, evil eyes stared out of the canvas. The pointed chin and forehead looked exaggerated but this was the thing from his dream. In the background was a tall figure, partly concealed in the fog. It was standing next to a stone circle which he knew were those at Marsham as he'd lived there as a child and had played there many times. He had cleverly concealed Runic symbols in his painting like he always had in the darker works. The eyes hid the most subtle of them. He had no idea why he hid the shapes in his bleaker paintings. Maybe one day he'd contact a psychologist to find out but that may reveal a side to his personality that he'd rather not discover. There must be a reason why his dreams were filled with such sinister themes. He'd thought those dark days were behind him.

As always when he'd finished one of these disturbing paintings he planned to get drunk. Expunge the black thoughts and wake up the next day with a nasty hangover but cleansed overall. He sat in his leather recliner and opened a bottle of vodka, not his usual tipple of expensive cognac but a cheap supermarket brand. He sipped from the bottle as he vaguely remembered the reason why his family had left Marsham. Something happened when he was a child. His family were forced to leave the village because of something he'd done. He remembered the blood on his hands and the strong coppery smell, and the horror on his mother's face as he held the dead cat up to her like an offering. It's eyes were missing. This time someone from the village had seen him. The family left for Salisbury soon after. They had already been shunned for months and the boy had to be kept away from school due to the rumours surrounding him. No one wanted him to spread his 'evil ways' to the other kids. A tear formed and ran down his cheek, rough after two days without shaving. He tilted the bottle back. His previous sips had turned to gulps of the fiery liquid. His memories became hazy as he slowly slipped into unconsciousness and the quarter full bottle dropped to the floor.

Behind his chair a small spotlight he used for reading turned itself on. The bulb glowed, became hotter by the second and then exploded, shards of white hot glass showering the carpet. Brand was oblivious to this. The carpet started to smolder, a patch of the beige carpet was rapidly beginning to turn a dark brown. The pungent smell of the melting synthetic fibres filled the air. The dark patch reached the spilt vodka and ignited it. In the corner of the room a dark shape watched and waited. It didn't take long for the fire to spread throughout the large house. The last room to be totally decimated by the flames was the studio. This portrait was never named.

Mark woke in pain again. Apart from the abating discomfort behind his eyeball both eyes were streaming with tears. He got out of bed and walked to the bathroom. He turned on the light and stared into the mirror. His eyes were red and watery like he'd been rubbing them. Maybe the pain was just him poking himself in his sleep? He certainly hoped so. Maybe the first two instances were real and the second two, while he was asleep, were him just dreaming about eye pain? Probably nothing to worry about, he thought.

That night Ellie had another dream. She'd been so hot she'd kicked off the duvet and was sweating even though it was the last night of April. In the dream she'd been paralysed, with flames all around her, the heat was unbearable, the smoke filling her lungs. She was slouched in a chair in a room she didn't recognise. She saw a dark shape in the the room about twenty feet away and realised it was a tall woman although she seemed misty and slightly unformed. The woman seemed to be shouting something in anger, enjoying the spectacle of the flames leaping around. Ellie felt no pain but she did feel panic and her legs started to blacken, the intense heat and smoke were somehow comforting because she knew it would all be over in a few seconds.

Ellie woke, sucking in the cool air of the bedroom and then coughing violently. She lay there, eyes wide, and remembered every detail of the dream. Why was this different to the ones set in the past? She got up, went to the bathroom and turned on the light. She looked in the mirror and saw her face was extremely red like she had a bad sunburn, Ellie filled a glass with water and gulped it down, then filled another and sipped it this time. The crimson on her cheeks and neck began to fade.

Friday May 1st

At work the next day Mark got a call from Sydney, everything was approved, credit checks and references were fine and he could move in as soon as he picked up the keys. Mark believed things were starting to look up after the last two weeks of misery. A home with Nat. Maybe the start of a family. Mark immediately texted Nat and his mum and told them he'd pick up the keys after work and move a few items into the new flat. It was another good day work wise, he'd made a fair number of sales and even with the break last week he'd make a lot in commission this month. Definitely improving, he thought to himself. A new chapter in his life.

His phone rang just as he'd stopped for lunch. It was Inspector Daly.

"What can I do for you Inspector," he asked.

"Do you know Dominic Brand, the artist?"

"Well, I don't actually know him exactly but I did call him a day or two ago to ask him about one of his paintings. I'd seen it in a gallery while I was away on that break. Why do you ask?"

"Mr Brand died in a fire last night and the local lads think it may be arson so, as a matter of course, they checked his phone records in case there were any threats and your number came up."

"God, that's terrible. As I said I called him about a painting and the inspiration behind it. All very amicable."

"I don't want you to take this the wrong way but there does seem to be a number of recent deaths with you as a connection. I understand your girlfriend's father is also missing and he's now presumed dead by the police in Aberdeen."

"It has to be coincidence. You know I wasn't there when Steve had his accident and I was long gone from the office when Paul hung himself and I was certainly nowhere near Dominic Brand when he died, arson or not. I've never even met him or Nat's dad either!"

"As I said to you before I've seen some strange thing over the years and I've heard some even stranger ones. I don't for a minute believe you have anything to do with the deaths directly but there is a connection in my mind. I don't believe in coincidence so as you can imagine I'm intrigued, especially if you add your break-in to the mix. I have to ask, do you know of anyone who would want to implicate you in these deaths?"

"No, I just can't see how they would do it anyway. Steve's dying was definitely an accident although he should have known better than work on a powered up lawn mower, Paul's death was suicide and it was my idea to phone the artist. Oh wait, I was given his number by a friend I'm doing some research with, Professor James Anderson, he teaches at the local college. I can't see him being the sinister type and he never knew Steve or Paul anyway as far as I know."

"Okay, the plot thickens as they say in those old mystery books. As you know I'm not involved with the cases of Brand or Natalie's father, and the suicide and accident are officially closed but I am keeping an eye on things in my spare time, not that a copper gets a lot these days with all the paperwork. I'll keep you updated if I hear anything as I'm sure you are as baffled by the connection as I am at the moment."

"Good to hear Inspector, thanks. Oh, by the way, do you know if the guys in Aberdeen have informed Nat that her dad is presumed dead now? She asked them to use her as the point of contact now."

"I'm not aware if they've contacted anyone further to the initial call to his ex-wife."

"I'm not sure if I should tell Nat he's presumed dead then."

"I wouldn't. After all, I haven't called you today, have I? He may still turn up anyway."

"I see your point, thank you, goodbye Inspector."

Mark was beginning to like Daly. He was as fascinated by the whole thing too. Was there a connection to him? He felt he should call Jim Anderson later, maybe even drop round. He doubted if Jim had even heard about Brand's death yet but Daly was sure to give Jim's name to the investigating officers in Salisbury, so he'd want to give Jim a heads up that he may get a call in the next few days. Why would someone want to kill Brand anyway? Maybe it was a robbery gone wrong or even a jealous husband. Maybe it was even suicide? He'd probably never know.

He'd decided not to say anything to Nat about her dad. If she'd heard anything she would have told him. He didn't want anything to spoil the look on her face when he dangled the flat keys in front of her after picking them up on the way to meet her after work. If she heard anything from the police then they'd deal with it.

The rest of the afternoon dragged a bit, the excitement of the new flat building up in him. At five o'clock he rushed to his car, drove to the estate agent and retrieved the keys from Sydney then went to pick Nat up.

As expected she beamed when she saw the keys and urged him to get going to the old flat and pick up a few things and then head straight over to the new place. They grabbed a few items and then were en route to Marsham village. The high street there was just starting to empty of cars so they had no trouble parking in front of the greengrocers and walked through the short alley to the iron stairs at the back. They quickly ascended them and Mark smiled as he put the key in the lock and turned it. The door swung open and the loud beeping panicked him. He'd forgotten about the alarm in his excitement. He fumbled through his wallet for the piece of paper Sydney had given him and entered the four digit number into the console just in time.

They moved straight into the kitchen and unloaded the cardboard box Nat carried. Kettle, tea bags, coffee, sugar and mugs. Just the essentials. They could pick up things like fresh bread and milk from the newsagents a few doors away. It was open until ten o'clock he remembered. He called Ellie and invited her and Jack to come round for their first cup of tea in the new place. Ellie told him they were about to leave and would be there in fifteen minutes. While they waited Mark nipped to the newsagents for milk and biscuits.

Ellie's excitement gradually faded as Jack drove near the stones. The panic of the previous day and her latest dream still fresh in her mind. She couldn't remember being so scared and alone in her life before and never wanted to experience what she did in that copse ever again. She certainly never wanted to visit the mystic circle on her own again. Jack reached the now quiet village and parked behind Mark's Jag. Nat was waiting for them and hugged them both, taking them through the short alley to the rear of the shop. Ellie was holding a bunch of daffodils that she'd picked up from a petrol station on the way over. She'd also brought a tall glass vase from home. She gave them both to Nat once they were inside and Nat filled the vase with water and arranged the flowers and put the vase in the centre of the kitchen table while Mark gave his parents the guided tour. By the time they'd returned Nat had poured and the tea was ready.

"It really is a lovely place," said Ellie, "I really love that bathroom."

"We love the whole place," replied Nat, "I can see us being happy here, it was great living with you two for a few days but our own place is something special."

"It is. I remember when Jack and I moved in together, we were as excited as you two are. You certainly have everything you need in the high street too, no need to go into town at all."

"I love the area, it's so peaceful," smiled Nat. The excitement in her voice was obvious and hard to contain, not that she'd want to anyway.

They were anxious to spend the night in their new home but decided to wait until the weekend as planned. Jack would book the van rental in the morning and they'd get an early start. There wasn't too much to move as the other flat had been furnished too, so they should have everything done by mid afternoon and Mark and Nat could spend their first night in their new home.

Mark followed Jack's Mercedes back to his parent's house and after they ate they settled in for the night with a few drinks, watching an old Bob Hope film, a murder mystery set in a creepy house surrounded by a swamp.

Later Nat was awakened by a persistent tapping at the bedroom window.

She couldn't see anything but fog through the glass. She got out of bed, trying not to disturb Mark and walked slowly to the window. She began to feel threatened and in danger somehow even though she was safely inside the house. She thought it could be a hailstorm but did they happen when it was foggy? Nat was no expert on the weather but didn't think so. There were no trees near the house so it couldn't be the end of a branch flicking the pane in a breeze. She couldn't see anything on the other side of the glass except the thick, cloying vapour. Maybe it was her imagination? It wasn't a dream, she was fully awake now, she could hear Mark snoring and then groan as he rolled over onto his injured arm. She went back to bed and tried to ignore the sound, imagining what it would be like to live in the new flat with Mark and maybe even start a family in a few years. She drifted off to sleep again with happy thoughts and plans for the future. Outside, a tall shape moved across the lawn in the gloom.

Saturday May 2nd

By morning Nat was still a little concerned. It was a total mystery the way she knew the tapping was there but there was no evidence as to what caused it. She then thought that she should have used her phone to record what was happening and then she'd at least know if it was her imagination or not. Weird things had been going on recently and most had no real explanation. She made breakfast for herself and Mark. Jack and Ellie weren't up yet. Probably sleeping off the drink they'd had last night. Ellie didn't work after her retirement and Jack was just part time at the accountants, advised by a doctor to try and take things a bit easier so only worked two or three days a week now and delegated most things. The perks of owning his own company.

She fancied a night out so called her best friend Erika and suggested a meal. Erika was itching to get out too, work was getting on top of her a bit and she needed to relax.

Jack appeared and had a quick coffee with some toast, raring to get on with the move. Mark dropped Nat off at work and he and Jack went to pick up the van Jack had rented for the day. They were given a Renault Kangoo, which despite the silly name, was perfect for the job. Mark insisted in calling it their Kangaroo and hoped there was plenty of room in the pouch for his vinyl record collection. Jack was reminded that however old your kids got there was still a little child in them at times.

They stopped off at the storage company in town and bought boxes, bubble wrap and tape then Jack followed Mark. They arrived at the old flat just before eleven and Mark thought they needed a nice mug of tea to set them up for the day then realised they'd taken everything to the new flat the day before. Jack said he'd walk down to the petrol station at the end of the road to get a couple of coffees while Mark made a start on putting the boxes together and play with the bubble wrap like a five-year-old.

Jack returned ten minutes later with a pair of large coffees and a couple of sausage rolls which he heated up in Mark's microwave. Sausage rolls devoured, they made a start on packing. Mark realised exactly how little he'd accumulated in the four years he'd lived in the flat. Mainly clothes and shoes went into the boxes as well as the expensive stereo and speakers Jack and Ellie had bought him for his records and CDs. The DVD player and around 50 discs in cases took up two boxes. The rest of the boxes were filled with tinned and packet food, everything from the bathroom was put in plastic bags to prevent leakage including cleaning products.

Kim had seen the Jag and the van parked outside the flat so came over for a chat. Everything was set for the funeral in two days and she was getting things ready for her mum and sons to arrive from Nottingham. Jack told her that if she ever needed financial advice to call him and not have to pay for it elsewhere. She thanked him and did say that she definitely would need some help in a week or two. There was just so much to sort out. She invited them over for a drink before they left for the new flat. Mark did one last walk through to check he hadn't missed anything they needed to take and he and Jack followed Kim to her house. She made them all a cup of tea and Mark stood and stared out of the patio window at the lawn where his best friend had died. Mark was silent, immersed in his thoughts while Jack and Kim made polite small talk.

Mark drove towards Marsham, Def Leppard screaming from the four speakers, and was singing along to *Animal* with Jack following in the van. As it was just Saturday afternoon the high street was busy but they found space in the car park behind the grocers and they started to unload the boxes and take them up the metal staircase, or rather Jack took the lightest of them up and Mark did all the legwork ferrying the boxes while Jack waited on the balcony in front of the door to the flat. Once inside they put the various boxes in their proper places, unpacked and sat in the kitchen while Mark put the kettle on. Mark needed a brew after all that running up and down the steps, his back beginning to ache dully. They left Mark's TV, DVD player and stereo in the van as he wouldn't need them there and Jack said he could store them in his garage.

"That wasn't too bad," said Jack. "Couple more hours putting things away and we'll have cracked it."

"I'll have to go a bit slowly, my back is playing up a bit."

"Well, you do the light stuff like the bathroom and I'll set up the front room and the bedroom then we do kitchen between us."

"Sounds good. Once we drop the van off and I get you home I'll pick Nat up from work and we can get her things from home, she'll just need her clothes for now and there is room in the Jag to store it until tomorrow. She texted me earlier and said she was going out with her friend Erika later so we'll spend the night at your place again and finish off with her things tomorrow."

"I've met Erika, haven't I? Mad as a bag of ferrets but all the best people are. Lovely girl."

"Yes, at a party in the old flat. I'm amazed we got so many people in there."

"It was pretty cramped to say the least," chuckled Jack. "There must have been thirty people in there at one point."

"We were lucky the floor didn't collapse and all of us join old Mrs. Evans in the flat below."

"That would have ruined her Saturday night in front of the TV." They both roared with laughter at the thought of crushing the X Factor judges.

They were done unpacking by about four which was pretty much perfect. They would have been finished sooner but Jack insisted on two more tea breaks, he was more like a factory shop steward than an accountant. The van was delivered back to the rental company and the remaining boxes transferred to the boot and back seat of the Jag and they were back at Jack's place just before five. Ellie had been cooking and gardening all day and had enjoyed the peace and quiet. Mark relaxed for a few minutes with a cold drink and then left to get Nat from work.

The atmosphere at Nat's mum's house was frosty at best and Mark gave up trying to make conversation while Nat was in her bedroom throwing most of her clothes and shoes into a couple of suitcases. Her toiletries went into a plastic bag and she was ready to go.

There were no good luck wishes from her mum, just a cold stare as Mark grabbed the cases. Nat was visibly upset and once in the car Mark tried to console her with a few kind words and told her that her mum would get used to the idea eventually. It would be the first time in her life that she'd ever been alone permanently so she would take a while to come round and accept Nat moving out. He told her that her mum needed to evolve and stop living in the past so much.

When they got back to Mark's parents house Nat quickly changed for her night out with Erika. Ellie had made lamb chops with rosemary and mash for the rest of them which Mark was dying to get his hands on but Ellie made him wait until after Nat left because it would be rude to eat in front of her.

After dinner they spent the evening relaxing and watching a couple of DVDs, *The African Queen* and an old SciFi called *The Day The Earth Caught Fire* with Leo McKern. Jack and Mark were sharing a nice bottle of single malt and were dozing before the planet was eventually saved. Ellie sipped her sweet white wine, totally engrossed in both films. She loved Bogart and had dozens of his films on DVD.

Erika had picked Nat up at around seven in her little yellow car she called Custard. She was wearing a pink sweatshirt and black jogging bottoms and white trainers. She was a little older than Nat, late thirties and was always trying to keep fit. Full faced and always smiling. She was happily married to Barry and lived in a suburb of London but not too far away. Erika used to work at Canary Wharf but then changed jobs and worked in Birmingham four days a week, staying in hotels and commuting on a Monday morning and a Thursday evening and working from home on a Friday. She loved her job but wasn't keen on the travel or being away from Barry for most of the week. Nat and Mark had travelled up to Birmingham by train to meet up with Erika for an evening meal a few months previously. After visiting a Tim Horton's coffee house and spending a couple of hours in the Birmingham Museum and Art Gallery, which was near New Street station where they had disembarked, Erika had met them and they made their way to Bill's diner which Nat thought was excellent.

They drove to Watford to Bill's diner there and sat in a booth trying to narrow down everything on the menu to a manageable amount. They'd also been to the Bill's in St. Albans, they loved the food. The waitress asked them if they were ready to order but they said they need more time and ordered a couple of pints of cider to help them decide. Eventually they decided and Nat chose Crispy Calamari while Erika went for Crumbed Halloumi sticks as starters. They also ordered their main course while they were at it, Erika wanted her favourite, Slow Cooked Beef Ribs which came in a red wine sauce with greens and chive mash. Nat thought she'd try something new, a Buttermilk Chicken Burger with fries and an interesting sounding coleslaw and chipotle mayonnaise.

"It's been way too long since we had a girlie night out, just the two of us," smiled Nat.

"We've both been busy, you have Mark now and your coursework to finish and I'm just snowed under with work at the moment."

"We should set up a foursome with Mark and Barry, invite you round to the new flat for a meal once we are settled, maybe in two or three weeks?"

"That would be great, I'm dying to see the new place, I've always like Marsham. So how's Mark?"

"He's taken Steve's death pretty hard even though he's being a typical bloke and trying to hide it. There was the suicide of his workmate too which was a bit of a shock. The break-in of course. And then he had an accident on his walk the other day."

"An accident? What happened? Is he okay?" asked Erika showing concern.

"He doesn't really know, most of it is still a blank but he was on his walk and the next thing he knows is he's running across a field and jumping over a gate and just passed out from the pain in his back. He somehow ripped his arm open on some rusty barbed wire too. Some girl found him and gave him a lift to Jack and Ellie's which is where we've been staying this week. I won't say what my first thought was when I saw him in her passenger seat."

"You've no worries there, Mark's a good bloke and wouldn't cheat on you. So are you excited about moving in together?"

The conversation paused as the waitress arrived with their starters, then left.

"Can't wait. I know it's been less than a year since we met but I really think we have something special. I just wish Mark would open up a bit about what *he* wants for a change. He says he only wants to make me happy."

"You say that like it's a bad thing," laughed Erika. Nat grinned.

"Sometimes he's just *too* nice, not like Stuart was."

Stuart had been an ex-boyfriend who was very self-centred and arrogant. He was a bit of a bad boy and always getting into trouble with the police. Like a lot of girls Nat was attracted to this belligerent image and his not caring about anything other than a night out with the lads. Nat realised that he really didn't care about her either and a couple of slaps from him during an argument confirmed that those type of people are really not worth the effort. She felt safe with Mark, and safe was by far the preferable option. The more she thought the more she realised that Mark really was the man for her.

Maybe she'd prefer him to be more ambitious and get a better job, one that stretched him, but at the end of the day it was his choice. He lived within his means and wasn't one of the 'I want it now' generation like so many of her friends. He hadn't run up debts on credit cards like a lot of them so she knew he was sensible about his finances. She supposed being the son of an accountant had helped a lot with his money management. Once she was a qualified psychotherapist she'd be earning good money. Enough for the both of them if need be.

Their main courses were excellent. They were both pretty full so decided to give the dessert a miss but did want to finish things off with something hot and boozy. No need to ask Erika what she wanted, Tia Maria coffee was her favourite after meal tipple and Nat went for a Boozy Hot Chocolate flavoured with Kahlua.

The conversation got round to Nat's mum and she told Erika about her dad going missing and how her mum was still bitter after all these years and what had happened earlier when Nat picked up some clothes.

"You know I love your mum but when I used to go round to your house she always scared me a bit. Like she was on the verge of exploding. It's a shame she never found someone else, found a bit of happiness for herself. I liked your dad though, he was always nice to me when he visited."

"I don't think she could find someone else. There would always be that fear of rejection in her mind and she'd never trust anyone else. She's destined to be alone for the rest of her life and no amount of telling her to find something or someone else to be a part of her life will do any good. She really upset me this afternoon with her total apathy towards my feelings and Mark's too so this would be a good time for us to actually spend a bit of time apart, let her think about what she did and her attitude in general towards other people and how she hurts them. No one has upset her other than my dad, so why take it out on everyone else?"

"That's the way some people are petal, they are so consumed by their own emotions that they rarely see what they are doing to others. I know you love her but leaving her be for a while may actually do her some good. Make her appreciate you a bit more."

The evening ended when Erika dropped Nat off at Mark's parent's place at about ten-thirty and they hugged goodbye. Erika drove off thinking she could hear wedding bells in the distance. She loved weddings."

Nat loved Erika like the sister she always craved, she had the most beautiful soul she had ever met. Erika was always there for her even if it was just on the end of a phone or even social media. Always reliable and talked sense. Always the first of her friends she turned to for advice or to pick her up emotionally. She really had to get that foursome arranged.

Erika drove into the light mist that was forming. Custard's headlights cutting into the thickening gloom. She hated driving in extreme weather like snow, hail and torrential rain but fog was the worst. She crawled at less than twenty along the country lanes, once or twice pulling into a passing point to allow a car coming from the opposite direction to get through. She was nearing Marsham when the mist became a thick fog. A right pea souper like they had before smokeless coal. She had to stop, it was just impossible to continue until it thinned out. She had managed to crawl into another short passing point and could hear the twigs of the hedge scrape along Custard's bodywork - Barry wouldn't be happy but better safe than sorry. No point in risking it so she sat in the car and left the engine running and made sure her fog and brake lights were lit so that people could see her if they were brave or stupid enough to still be driving. She turned on the radio and got nothing but static so slipped a CD into the player to relieve her loneliness and encroaching anxiety. If she had any idea what Mark, Nat or Ellie had experienced recently she wouldn't be sitting in her car all alone. She'd be inching along the road trying to find an end to the fog. She thought about leaving the car and walking into Marsham and finding shelter in a pub but knew that would be totally idiotic, if a car came along they wouldn't see her and she'd end up like a hedgehog, squashed in the middle of the lane. No, she was in the safest place and the fog must clear soon … she hoped. She decided to call Barry to tell him she'd be late home, as soon as the fog lifted she'd be on her way again. She even took a picture with the phone to show him how bad it was.

Erika heard a light tapping from the rear of the car, she thought at first it was wind moving a twig but realised if there was any sort of wind it would have moved the fog too. What was it? Maybe an animal? A hedgehog reading her earlier thoughts and going for some sort of sick retribution? *Revenge Of The Offended Hedgehogs* sounded like a really bad fifties horror film. She turned the volume up on the stereo and started to sing. Her voice faltering in places as she started to shiver. The temperature had dropped rapidly, she adjusted the heat control to full hot in the car but it didn't seem to make much difference. Her bare hands felt like ice. It was May for God's sake, not the depths of winter in a Russian Gulag. She checked the glove box to see if she'd left a pair of gloves in there but no luck. Erika tried to think positive thoughts. Nat's possible wedding for a start, she'd love to see her best friend married, happy and starting a family. Next spring would be nice. She liked Mark a lot and she knew he was really good for her. More tapping from the rear. She turned the volume up even more. She was safe in her car, she checked the central locking just in case then huddled up inside her coat. It had a fur collar so she buried her face into it, imagined she was cocooned in a nice warm place. Safe. Happy thoughts. Please.

There was a banging on her driver's side window, a dark face peered into the car, mouthing words at her. She hit the button to wind down her window.

"Fall asleep did we?" said the burly black policeman suspiciously.

"There was thick fog, I pulled in here. It was too dangerous to drive."

"We've had no reports of fog in this area, have you been drinking?"

"I went out for a meal earlier and had a pint of cider, but that was…" She looked at her watch and it was gone 4 am. "More than eight hours ago! I've been here since about eleven o'clock. It was really foggy." She then thought to show him the photo she'd taken earlier to send to Barry.

"You'd better be on your way," he said satisfied, "Have you got far to go?"

"Only about ten more miles, I'd better called my husband to tell him I fell asleep, he'd be worried sick."

She called Barry who had been waiting up for her and wasn't far off ringing the hospital as he'd been unable to get through to her phone. He wasn't happy but said he would be waiting for her and would put the kettle on. Luckily he had a couple of days off so he could make up the missed sleep. The police car started to drive down the lane and Erika slowly followed.

Sunday May 3rd

Mark and Nat were up early to get breakfast before the remainder of their move. Just coffee and toast for the present. Ellie wasn't up yet but she'd be going with them to help out and provide another feminine touch to the new place.

"Excited?" asked Mark as he buttered his toast.

"Bloody hell, yes," replied Nat. "And nervous, it's a big step for us."

"Look, you've stayed over enough times and we've had weekends and holidays together so the getting on part will be easy. The financial side of living together will be a change for both of us, a proper partnership."

"Should we get a joint bank account?"

"I think we should, and pay all the bills from it. It would probably help our credit rating too and maybe it would be easier to get a mortgage in the future."

"The future. I like the sound of that," she smiled.

"Good morning, my dears," said Ellie as she appeared in the kitchen doorway. "I assume you two are looking forward to your first real home?"

"We were just discussing finances, and how much of a change it would be. Having to consider the other person before spending money or making decisions."

"That is a big step for anyone, I know we struggled to get used to it at first. Makes you a lot more responsible," said Ellie.

"Remember my mate Dave? When he was married his wife spent money like water. He was buying his clothes at Primark while she spent a hundred quid on a pair of shoes, she went out and spent five hundred on a computer desk for their flat without even telling him. He just couldn't plan for anything, there was no trust."

"I know Nat well enough to say she wouldn't be an idiot like Dave's ex," replied Ellie as she poured water from the just boiled kettle onto her herbal tea. "I'd have to turn into an evil mother-in-law," she grinned wickedly.

"No chance of either of those things," said Nat. "I intend for us to save as much as we can for the future. And you haven't got an evil bone in your body, I know you pretty well too," she smiled.

"Aren't you having something to eat mum?" asked Mark.

"Too excited!" beamed Ellie. "I'll be ready to go whenever you two are."

Ten minutes later they were leaving in the Jaguar with Nat clutching the keys to the new flat, eager to see what progress Mark and Jack had made the previous day. Gary Moore's bluesy *Movin' On* was aptly playing as they left. They passed the dell Mark had visited a few days ago on their left. Mark still felt a bit uneasy about the episode, mainly due to the lack of memory of what had happened. Why couldn't he remember? Why had he run? What scared him so much he'd risked his back injury to get away? They quickly passed the dell and Mark's uneasiness faded gradually the further away they travelled.

Marsham seemed like it was deserted but Mark supposed it was like this every Sunday morning. The newsagents were open and the pub would open a bit later but there was no sign of anyone in the high street. Mark thought he would love the peace and quiet, especially after the late Saturday nights in the flat in the future. They parked directly outside the greengrocer again and made their way through the alley and up the black iron stairs to the flat. Mark had taken Nat's suitcases from the boot and carried them in. He was ready to disable the alarm this time and was first through the door to put the suitcases in the large bedroom while Nat and Ellie entered the kitchen to inspect the work of Jack and Mark the day before. They approved. Mark returned and they had a quick cup of coffee before they got started. Nat then put her clothes away in the bedroom's wardrobes while Mark put away her cosmetics and toiletries in the spacious bathroom cabinets and Ellie did some general tidying up in the front room while listening to the radio on the stereo system.

Jack arrived at about eleven with four carrier bags full of groceries which he'd picked up from a supermarket close to town and then invited them to lunch as soon as they were finished with the final details of the move. They walked to the pub a little way down the street which had just opened and ordered their meals, while they waited Mark and Jack sipped pints of real ale and Ellie had diet coke while Nat chose a lager and lime. Jack fancied the shepherds pie and mixed veg, Mark the roasted rack of lamb with broccoli and spinach, chicken and mushroom pie and mash for Nat and Ellie the asparagus and ricotta ravioli which she had really enjoyed when Jack had taken her there for dinner a few months previously. For desert Mark and Nat devoured a serving of banoffee pie each and both Jack and Ellie wolfed down Bramley apple pie with vanilla ice cream and a raspberry sauce.

During the meal the conversation turned to local history. Ellie suggested they all go to Verulamium Museum in St. Albans for the afternoon as they hadn't been there for a couple of years and Nat had never been so was enthusiastic at the idea. She'd always been fascinated by mosaics since they studied the Romans in junior school, it was her favourite period of history.

The journey in Jack's Mercedes took less than thirty minutes. They got to the car park in front of the curious rounded facade of the museum and could see the remnants of the Roman wall situated across the park in the distance. Jack paid for the parking and left the ticket on the dashboard above the steering wheel and they all strolled towards the red building. They bought their tickets in the foyer and entered the showrooms of exhibits. There were vast displays of pottery, glassware, statues and metalwork from the period and also a large array of coins of all shapes and sizes. Nat thought the various life sized enactments of daily life were very good, the mannequins pretty lifelike, a carpenter planing some wood, a woman preparing a meal and another woman and a child doing what looked like spinning yarn for cloth.

Jack particularly liked an exhibit that told of Queen Boudicca burning Verulamium to the ground, as well as London and Colchester, around 60 A.D. He wasn't aware that her revolt stretched this far East so was pleased he'd learnt something new even though he'd been there before. He mused about what Britain would be like if she'd managed to drive the Romans back into the sea instead of being eventually defeated.

What impressed Mark were the open tombs on display housing skeletons which he assumed were real. Nat thought they were a bit creepy and realised that they were once living, breathing people. She wondered who they were and what they did, who were their families? Did they die of natural causes and at what age or did they die in battle, killed by a native raiding party? History is full of mystery.

Ellie loved the bronze statue named the 'Verulamium Venus', a topless woman, thought by a lot of scholars to be the Queen of the Underworld, Persephone holding a pomegranate.

The most impressive and amazing exhibits of all were the mosaics, all dating from around 180 A.D. They were built inside a large town house and still remarkably preserved. There was one supposedly of a sea shell but Nat thought it looked more like a sunrise over rolling hills. It was perpendicular, which added to the sunrise perception, and was lit by four spotlights from underneath There was an intricate mosaic of a lion and a stag with very fine borders and another of a dahlia in a central rectangle with other four sided panels separated by what looked like rope or chains. This one had a couple of large parts missing. The best of all was of a figure not unlike the one on the back of Mark's amulet. A slightly demonic figure which represented a sea god, possibly Neptune the God of the Oceans or Fontus who represented wells and springs. The outer parts were inlaid by a maze-like structure and also contained chalices and flowers so Mark thought Fontus would be the most likely candidate.

They'd spent nearly two hours admiring everything there as well as taking hundreds of pictures between them so thought it was time for some fresh air. After browsing the gift shop quickly without buying anything they walked out of the front of the building and through the car park to Verulamium Park which held a large lake, home to several types of water birds, including an island for some herons. The lake had a wide path around it where people walked, with and without dogs, and jogged in various shades of spandex. On their right were the remains of a Roman wall which was fenced off by black iron railings to protect the two thousand year old structure from the hands of the curious and the souvenir hunters. From where they stood near the wall they could see the cathedral towering on top of a steep hill. They walked around the lake taking pictures of the various birds either flying or floating on the lake. Nat wished she had some bread to feed the ducks.

It was still fairly early in the afternoon so they walked to the remains of the Amphitheatre near the museum. Built around 140 A.D. it was a large site that housed an area with seating for dancing, wrestling, armed combat and also religious events. It was the only one of it's type ever built in Britain as it had a stage. Only a few crumbling walls, some steps and a column still remained there. After constant redevelopment, by 300 A.D, it could seat 2000 spectators . The whole site only took about twenty minutes to walk round which was a little disappointing as they had paid to get in.

Jack saw a sign that the site was owned by the Gorhambury Estate and was reminded of some other ruins he'd not been to in over twenty years and was nearby, on the way back to Marsham. They walked back to the car and Jack drove less than a mile to the entrance to the estate. A long tree-lined country lane with many speed bumps and flanked by pastures took them to a fork, the left one went to the new Gorhambury House, a palatial building built in 1777 and the subsequent seven years by Sir Robert Taylor, the same man who built the Bank of England. The right hand road twisted around to a ruined building surrounded by fields on three sides and a thick expanse of trees on the fourth. It was built by Sir Nicholas Bacon, father of the more famous Francis, during the reign of Elizabeth I. They walked amongst the ruins for several minutes. There wasn't much left but you could walk through and get a feeling for the place. They all noticed the mist coming through the trees and the temperature had dropped. Mark felt very nervous, a fragment of what happened in the dell coming back to him. He was very relieved when Jack said it was probably time to make a move as he didn't fancy feeling his way over invisible speed bumps getting out of the estate. Ellie felt a lot better about leaving as well but kept her silence. Nat remembered the tapping at the bedroom window too. They drove back down the lane, keeping well ahead of the cloudy vapour. Three of them in deep thought.

They got back to Mark and Nat's flat and decided to get a Chinese from the place in the high street. Mark and Jack walked down and browsed the menu and ordered for the four of them. Maybe a bit too much but you can never have too much they thought. Leftovers heated in the microwave were always pretty good. A small, dark haired woman in a blue bib overall took their order and Mark paid with his debit card and she said it would be ready in 20 minutes so they nipped over the road to the pub for a quick pint.

"That fog was a bit weird up at Gorhambury," remarked Jack.

"I've been seeing quite a lot recently, maybe there is something in this climate change stuff?"

"We never used to get so much, there is usually some trace most mornings when I get up now. Temperatures are all over the place too. Did you notice the drop when we saw that fog?"

"Yes, definitely some strange things going on. When we saw that fog at Gorhambury a bit of what happened when I had my accident the other day came back, not much though."

"What do you remember?" asked Jack.

"I was in the dell and there was a lot of fog drifting down into the hollow and I must have panicked or something so I scrambled up the incline and tried to get over the barbed wire and that is where I cut myself, then sprinted across the field."

"So it was the fog that scared you? Just got a bit spooked?"

"Seems so, maybe there was an animal scratching around in there, a fox or a badger, and I just freaked out a bit," said Mark, slightly embarrassed.

"That will bloody well teach you not to go running across a field at full pelt. How is your back now?"

"Not too bad, still a bit stiff and my wrist feels like it's healing pretty well too."

Jack looked at his watch. "You ready to make a move?"

They both drained their pint glasses, said goodnight to the short white man with a strange ginger afro behind the bar, and ambled across the road to the takeaway.

"That was some afro, you'll probably see a lot of him now you know," Jack laughed.

"You have my permission to shoot me if I ever get a haircut like that, he looked like a stunted white dandelion."

They were still laughing when they entered the takeaway, the woman behind the counter looking at them like they were a bit mad. Mark took the three white plastic bags from the woman and he and Jack set off for the flat.

They sat watching a DVD while sharing their sweet and sour chicken, chili beef, beef curry and pork in black bean sauce accompanied by a lot of rice and noodles. To compliment their Roman excursion Mark put Gladiator on. Not Ellie's cup of tea but she didn't object to watching Russell Crowe in a skirt. Jack and Ellie left around ten to give Mark and Nat a chance of an early night and relax before the funeral the next day.

Monday May 4th

It was a bright, sunny morning when the two shining black cars arrived at the crematorium, the rest of the mourners parked at a nearby supermarket rather than spend £2.50 at the council run car park even further away. The hearse moved around to the back of the building while the limo parked outside the front entrance and Kim, her mum and the two boys, all dressed in black, solemnly got out and moved slowly up the steps to the large structure. The other mourners moved in single file along the path from the car park, mostly in silence. Around forty people had turned out to pay their respects and support Steve's family.

As people filed into the service area they sat in the rows of padded seats. Steve's family were already seated at the front, staring at the coffin in which he was contained. Obviously no open casket in this service due to what happened to him. Everyone seated, the service started. Robert Johnson's *Crossroads* seeped out from hidden speakers in the walls as the local priest walked to the centre of the hall. Mark had no idea Steve was a Catholic. They had never talked about religion in all the years they had known each other. Football and music were the staples of conversation since they had been friends. The priest led the prayers and said a few comforting words. He had complied with Kim's wishes that the service shouldn't be too religious as Steve wasn't that religious in his later years and hadn't attended Mass for a long time. It was time for the second of the songs Kim had chosen with the help of Mark. *The Sky Is Crying* by Elmore James filled the room. When it was over Mark got up and walked stiffly to the podium. Kim had asked Steve's best friend to say a few words because she had been unable to stand up and do it herself, afraid she would break down and become a total mess.

"I'm more used to speaking over the phone to faceless people rather than addressing an audience. I feel like a bad stand-up comedian who knows he'll never get a laugh in a month of Sundays so I'll make this short." The congregation tittered politely.

"Anyway, I've known Steve for a good few years, we never met at school or playing sports when we were younger though. We actually met in a pub during a televised football game between my team and his and as the drink flowed so did the banter. Good natured funny things like banter is supposed to be like. No threats of violence or crudeness or anything like that. I immediately liked him, but so did everyone who met him. He was a funny bloke that everyone loved. No airs or graces, he was himself, nothing fake. I don't think anyone can say anything different about him. He'd do anyone a favour if asked. From fixing a car to helping with decorating, he'd be the man to turn to. We spent a lot of time together, going to football, going to gigs, even just having a kick about in the park with his boys or chilling with a pint. If those lads grow up to be half the man he was then their mum will be more than happy and very proud. I remember about a year ago we went to a Black Star Riders gig in London and we got really drunk and ended up sleeping in a churchyard. Steve woke in the night and hid behind a gravestone and started to throw little bits of green marble at me while I slept and then I woke up and he jumped out at me. He was that sort of bloke, a really good laugh and he'll be missed by everyone who ever met him. I think the one thing that everyone will remember about him is that he loved Kim and the boys with all his heart. That's me done, thanks for listening."

Mark smiled sheepishly as people nodded at the last statement about Steve and he made his way back to his seat as the Muddy Waters classic *I'm Ready* filled the air. He looked up before he seated himself and saw Inspector Daly standing at the back in a dark suit and tie and wondered what he was doing there.

The wake was being held in the village hall, caterers were booked to provide the food and a local pub had provided all the drinks at cost price. A large framed photo of Steve in his beloved Arsenal shirt was displayed on an easel with bunches of flowers either side in the corner of the hall. Two trestle tables were covered in buffet food and another had bottles and cans of beer and bottles of red and white wine and soft drinks for the kids and about a hundred clear plastic cups were stacked and waiting to be filled. The guests started to drift in to the hall in small groups. Some had picked their children up on the way back from the crematorium and warned them to be on their best behaviour. It was half term so none were at school. Mark and Nat arrived and started to mingle, swapping memories and thoughts about Steve. Eventually Kim and the family arrived. They'd been back to the house to change into something a little less dour as the wake was a celebration of Steve's life and not a goodbye like it was at the crematorium. Steve's boss, Mick, appointed himself in charge of the music, Oasis seemed to be his favourite band as he played them rather too much. He mixed in a bit of Abba and Celine Dion too. At least Steve got to listen to some of his favourites at his own funeral unlike the wake. He'd have hated the Celine Dion.

People drifted in and out of the hall, most going for a quick smoke outside, some off home after a free lunch at the wake. Mark and Nat stayed close to Kim in case she needed them, Mark feeling very protective of his best friend's wife. Kim told Mark she'd like to be back home so he took her and the rest of her family back while Nat remained at the hall. Her friend Erika had arrived a few minutes earlier and Erika was telling her about the strange experience in the fog the other night. Nat stayed silent about her own exposure to the fog at the bedroom window and the mysterious tapping she heard. She was just relieved Erika got home safely in the end.

Erika said to Nat that she'd give her a lift home in Custard and it would be a good excuse to see the new flat. Nat called Mark to tell her she'd meet him at home. Erika arrived in Marsham high street about twenty minutes later and Nat took her up to their new home and gave her the guided tour. They sat in the front room listening to music and sipping wine when Mark returned. Mark joined them with a beer and reassured

Nat that Kim was home and seemed fine although still not fully herself. It would take a while he thought. Erika couldn't make the funeral due to work so Nat filled her in with details of the service and gushed about Mark's 'lovely speech' that was so heartfelt by everyone.

Nat made a simple meal of steak pie, chips and baked beans for the three of them which they ate at the kitchen table as the sun slowly went down over the copse hiding the stone circle. Erika left around nine and took the long way round, using the bypass instead of the lanes this time. She was still a bit unnerved about her trip home on Saturday night and didn't want to worry Barry again like she had before.

Detective Inspector Gerry Daly had been pulling intel from the National Crime Database in his office. It was nine-thirty and very few people were around on the top floor he shared with several other inspectors and their teams. He'd prefer to do his research at home but logging on from outside the building would be flagged up somewhere and he didn't want that.

Every case the police were involved with had it's own file and he was cross-referencing information to do with the four cases he was interested in: The gardening accident of Steven Jones, the apparent suicide of Paul Lomax, the possible arson and death involving the artist Dominic Brand and the disappearance of Michael Cross in Scotland. He was sure there was some sort of connection other than Mark Mason. The database searched with an algorithm looking for key words they had in common in their profile or reports and then the screen flashed and he smiled. All four were born in Marsham. As he'd told Mark he didn't believe in coincidence but although the connection was there he couldn't see a reason why their place of birth had anything to do with their deaths, or in the case of Cross, disappearance, although he was sure Cross was already dead. Some sort of crime ring going back decades? Unlikely. Jones was as straight as they come according to Mark Mason and the Lomax boy was just a kid living with his parents. Brand and Cross had moved away at least twenty years ago. He doubted any of them knew each other. There must be something else.

That evening Mark called Jim Anderson.

"Hi Jim, I thought I'd let you know that I got a call from the police. I don't know if you've heard or not but that artist Dominic Brand was killed in a fire a couple of nights ago and they think it may have been arson so they checked his phone records for possible threats and discovered I'd rung him. I told them you gave me his number so they may call you to verify that, I hope that's okay."

"My God. Another death! I was going to call you this evening with some news of my own. I have a friend who is really into Saxon lore and legend, the sort of thing that is passed down by word of mouth and not written down anywhere. He says that this Kendra Watkin was a healer but then was falsely accused of the murder and sacrifice of a young girl and branded a witch and was burnt at the stake for it. He says that her grandmother was a dark witch and had taught her some really potent magic including bringing herself back from the dead. It would involve a personal possession being secreted somewhere for someone to find and then the spell would be activated.

I hate to say this but I think the amulet was that possession, it would have had it's own residual power as it was taken from a sacred stone and 'the six' would be sacrificed in order to bring her back from the dead. When you found her stone talisman you may have activated the spell. Six will die, and there have been three since you found it, right?"

"Four, Nat's dad is missing, presumed dead," sighed Mark.

"Could this actually be happening for real, Mark? Is it really possible?"

"Jesus, if it is it's a nightmare and it's all my fault."

"It's only speculation at the moment, maybe it's just a story, a folk tale to scare children."

"I really hope so. I don't want any deaths on my conscience."

"If it is true then someone would probably have found the amulet eventually."

"But it was me and now I wish I hadn't, can I be responsible for Steve's death?"

"You didn't kill him. Either it was an accident or something else, but definitely not you. Get some rest tonight. I'll keep digging and call you."

Jim ended the call and hoped for everyone's sake that it wasn't real. He hadn't told Mark everything.
Later that night Stuart Pearson was in his tent in the middle of the dig on the Isle of Sheppey. He'd been sitting outside for a couple of hours listening to the wild wind and sipping brandy from the silver hip flask he always kept on him but it had got a little colder so decided to get in the tent to warm up a bit. The four students working with him were in the nice warm pub having a few beers before they retired to their rooms for

the night. Hopefully they wouldn't get too drunk, he didn't want to have to motivate them too much in the morning and he shouldn't need to after the momentous day they'd had. It had been a really excellent day. They'd uncovered a fairly intact Saxon shield buried in the deep, dark earth which normally would have been a great find, but it was what was underneath the shield in it's hollow that was why the students were celebrating over in the pub down the road tonight. A helmet, amazingly preserved, was made from iron and bronze and was inlaid with gold and silver around the guard that covered the face. Inside the helmet was a small wooden carving of a horse, possibly a child's toy, and that was the mysterious part for Stuart. The helmet and shield obviously belonged to someone of great importance, but was the toy a keepsake they had carried in memory of a dead child? It was nearing dark when they'd found the three artifacts but they would dig deeper in the morning to see if this was a burial and maybe even get some clue as to the identity of the owner. A burial was the more likely scenario as he couldn't see these things just hidden or lost in battle. They would have been taken. Stuart hoped they would even find a complete sword a little lower down. That would pose even more questions and a bigger mystery that would be virtually impossible to solve. He would get the helmet and shield packed up in the morning and one of the students could call a courier to get it shipped to the university. He never felt the need for a mobile phone of his own, too many distractions while he was on a dig. He was never a fan of technology and rarely used ground penetrating radar on his digs unless there was a real need. He was proud of probably being one of the last of the 'old school' archaeologists in the country.

He took another sip of the dark brandy, the glow from his kerosene lamp inside the tent glinting off the silver surface of the flask. It really was getting colder, much colder than previous nights and his famous poncho wasn't really keeping the cold out. He hoped there wouldn't be a drastic change in the weather that would delay tomorrow's excavation, not when there were possible answers inches below the spot they'd found the Saxon metalwork. He reminded himself he still got the same excitement during a find as he did when he was a student forty years ago. This could really be the swan song to cap his academic career.

He heard a slight scraping noise in the distance, thinking nothing of it he returned to the paperback he was reading, an old Shaun Hutson called *Relics.* He enjoyed horror books, a great bit of escapism. Maybe the noise was the owner of the helmet digging himself out of his grave? Stuart snickered to himself, the laugh somehow sounded empty inside the tent. He could now see his breath ghosting in front of his face. He'd seen snow in early May on a couple of his digs before throughout the years but never this close to the coast. He unzipped the opening of the large tent and stuck his head out. A very dense fog faced him, visibility of less than two feet. He wouldn't like to be out on the water tonight. He felt sorry for the fishermen out there, things were dangerous enough in their job without a fog like this and hoped it didn't go out too far to sea. He stood and walked a few paces and then he felt the need to sit on the cold mud near the spot they'd found that day's treasure. He absentmindedly scooped a handful of the damp earth and stuffed it into his mouth and chewed, mouthful followed mouthful, his stomach eventually full, grains of peaty sludge were drawn into his lungs. Over and over he scooped it into his mouth until he began to choke. No one was there in his final moments as his old heart failed.

In the fog a gravelly voice whispered, "She will return."

Anrok looked down on the prone figure in front of him. He would soon be released from the witch who called upon him and would wait in the fog until called again. He'd been invoked many times since almost the dawn of time itself. He was over eight feet tall and had a muscular grey body, his back covered in course black hair. Four thick black horns swept back from his wide forehead, his long nose and chin protruding from his face with a set of sharp fangs in between. His arms ended in giant claws. A long gold chain hung around his neck. From it dangled his own amulet, it looked like a wheel with a dark red eye in the middle surrounded by flames. It was this which gave him the power to force his victims to take their own lives. He had never shed a drop of blood himself although he was physically well equipped to do so with ease. Times had changed over the countless millennia and he had learnt to become more creative when it came to killing. He'd enjoyed that last one.

Mark had just fallen asleep when he started choking, a disgusting earthy taste in his mouth, and this time the pain behind his left eye took longer to recede. He'd woken Nat with his coughing this time too. She jumped out of bed and went to get him a glass of water from the kitchen. Nat returned and asked him if he was alright and held the glass to his lips. He gulped the water greedily trying to eradicate the taste more than anything else. He admitted that he'd been having more pains behind his eye since the first one in the car and promised he'd make an appointment with his GP. She looked worried and wondered why he'd kept all this from her. They'd only just moved in together and now she was thinking he didn't really trust her. It took her nearly two hours to get back to sleep again.

Tuesday May 5th

Mark was at work the next day and it was going pretty well considering the incident in the night, four new contracts sold and he was feeling good about his commission for this month already. Just after one o'clock his mobile vibrated in his pocket and it was Gerry Daly again.

"Hi Mark, is it a good time?" Mark thought that using his first name was a good sign and he wasn't a suspect anymore.

"Yes, just breaking for lunch."

"Fancy a pint? I have something you'll be interested in."

"Okay, where?" asked Mark.

"The Dragon is a short walk from where you are, isn't it? I'm already there."

"I'll be there in five minutes."

Mark ended the call, interested by whatever Daly had to say. His pace was brisk and he undercut his estimate by almost a full minute. Daly was standing at the bar with a full pint of lager in front of him, it was obviously his second ... at least.

"What are you drinking?" Daly asked.

"I'll have a Stella, if you don't mind."

When Mark had got his drink and taken a sip they went to sit in a booth at the back of the pub, away from anyone who may want to eavesdrop.

"Sounds like you had some free time to do your private detective thing," said Mark.

"Yes, I've been using the police database to try and find a connection behind all those deaths, other than you of course," Daly grinned, looking pleased with himself after the uncharacteristic blast of humour.

"So you did find another connection or I wouldn't be here."

One word did come up on the search algorithm, Marsham."

"Marsham?" said Mark with surprise.

"Yes, they were all born there, Brand, Lomax, your friend Steve and your girlfriend's father. All born in Marsham. They all moved eventually and two of them not too far away, but that's what I found."

"And you don't think it's a coincidence?"

"I keep telling you, I don't believe in coincidence, but I do believe in connections. There is a commonality there and for some reason people born in Marsham are dying in mysterious ways, individually not so strange, but as a collective there is a pattern and they *are* connected. The question is why? Who or what is killing them? And that brings to mind two things, motive and how they are doing it. Let's look at how first. Brand was possibly murdered by arson, simple enough it seems. The guy you worked with, Lomax, was definitely hung, the post-mortem confirms that but, and this is a big but, if someone asphyxiated him and then hung him on the door to make it look like suicide then how the hell did they get out? The office is on the third floor so the windows are out and there is no other exit. A classic locked room mystery unless he's bloody Spiderman."

"Maybe someone hypnotised him to hang himself?" suggested Mark.

"That's a possibility and for now we have nothing better."

"We?"

"I'm sure we'd do better if we worked together on this, I know you are as interested as I am in solving this. You knew two of them well, so can provide some insight. I have the resources."

"So are you Starsky or Hutch?" joked Mark.

"Keep that up and you can be Scooby Doo," laughed Daly.

"Okay, as long as we are honest with each other and don't hide anything."

"Fair enough, let's get back to things. We can't really speculate on Natalie's father because we don't know he's dead for sure but my gut feeling says he is, given the connection to the other three. Your friend Steve. Apparently a lawn mower accident. You said yourself that he was savvy enough not to work on a powered up mower. I think you are right there. Now did someone just walk up to him and force his head into the blades? I don't think so."

"Hypnotism again?"

"A possibility that could be a pattern. Was Brand hypnotised to maybe start his own fire? Now you have a definite paradigm. If not actual hypnotism then a definite influence like mind control."

"Does that even exist?"

"I thought everyone watched those conspiracy videos on Youtube."

"Just rock videos for me, I'm afraid," said Mark sheepishly.

"You've obviously heard of brainwashing but things like manipulation, thought reform, coercive persuasion? The sort of things the media are trying to use to promote their agendas. To persuade the population to follow a single narrative."

"Never really thought of it that way, Gerry. It does seem that we only get one side of the story these days and speculation is marketed as fact. I see lots of 'could have, may have and appears to be' in news reports."

"Exactly, I'm thinking it's possible it's a form of telepathy, someone willing the victims to kill themselves?"

"Makes sense, but who?" asked Mark.

"That's where motive comes in, Mark. If we knew why then we may better understand who."

"What if the motive isn't about *who* has died specifically, but what they represent or the type of people they are? They are all male, that's just too general though. Why the Marsham connection? Are all men born in Marsham potential victims?"

"On the face of it, yes, it's possible, but I don't think that's the real reason, it's something far deeper than that," said Daly.

They had both finished their drinks and Mark went to the bar for refills piecing together things in his mind. He paid with his card, brought the cold pints over, and sat down again. They sat and swallowed a few mouthfuls of the cold lager while both thought about the situation.

"So basically what we have is a female serial killer using telepathy to make men born in Marsham kill themselves?" said Mark.

"Sounds ridiculous when you say it that way, doesn't it?" shrugged Daly.

"Actually it may not be that far fetched. I'd need to speak to Jim Anderson before I say any more."

"Okay," Daly stood up and drained the remainder of his pint, "Speak to him and call me later, you have my number?"

"It's in my phone contacts."

"Talk to you later." Daly walked unsteadily to the door and Mark wondered if the detective was okay to drive.

That evening Jack and Ellie were round at the flat and they'd ordered pizza from a place in town that delivered and were having a nice relaxing evening.

While they were waiting Mark went to the bedroom and called Jim. The professor sounded very upset and maybe a little drunk.

"Hi Mark, I'm convinced we've had a fifth victim of the amulet, or rather, Kendra Watkin. It's real I'm afraid."

"What happened?"

"I got a call from the police today but it wasn't the reason you thought they'd call. My friend Stuart Pearson, dear old Poncho, died last night. Another bizarre death." He blinked back the tears.

"I'm so sorry Jim. He was the guy you went to visit last week wasn't he? At the dig?"

"Yes, we'd been friends for over twenty years since he was my tutor at Canterbury. He always camped at his digs to save the university money so he was all alone. All the students were billeted in the pub about half a mile away. Apparently he committed suicide by eating the earth from around the dig and eventually it got into his lungs. No post-mortem yet, but they think he may have had a heart attack before he suffocated. Given all the other deaths I certainly don't believe it was suicide. He was looking forward to retirement after this dig was over."

"Christ, that's terrible. I don't think it was suicide either. The reason I was calling was I had a meeting with Inspector Daly today. He believes that something is not right with all these deaths and is investigating on his own in his spare time. He used the police database to try and find a connection linking all four victims."

"Five now," interrupted Jim.

"Yes, five but he doesn't know about your friend, or he didn't when I saw him. Anyway, the first four victims, and I'm counting Nat's dad here, were all born in Marsham."

"Oh my God!" exclaimed Jim, "Stuart was born in Marsham too. He moved away when he went to Durham university and then on to Canterbury."

"Well, that seems to settle the connection. Five people all born in Marsham and all five dead in mysterious circumstances assuming Nat's dad is dead of course. One theory we came up with was that someone was willing these people to kill themselves."

"It makes sense. Watkin needs six sacrifices to come back to life. Her mental powers must be immense for her to retain them for fifteen hundred years and draw on the power from the amulet after it was found to infect the will of the victims like that. The demon, Anrok is forcing them to sacrifice themselves for her, she still has the power to control him."

"So what happens if she gets her sixth?" asked Mark.

"Mark, when I told you about the story of Watkin that was passed down through the generations I didn't tell you about the part where she got her power from a stone circle. The story says that even though she got her power from the stones they could also destroy her but it didn't say how. It also said that after each sacrifice she would begin to become more tangible, more solid. Almost complete, and complete enough to commit the last sacrifice herself. And that would be the end of the ritual to bring herself back fully, and also to give her everlasting life. What scares me is what she will do when she is immortal. What does she do with all that power when she'd be so untouchable? After being burnt at the stake for something she didn't do there would be a lot of rage there and revenge would be on her mind. Also your break-in makes sense now, she wanted the amulet back so no one can use it against her."

"You're right, I never even thought of connecting her and the break-in. I feel so stupid. I even thought I heard the phrase a couple of times too. So one will be safe even after the sixth victim?"

"She would rule... everything. Life on this planet would change forever. She would control all we know and what she didn't like or want she would destroy. We need to stop her, Mark. I'd appreciate it if you were in possession of the amulet, so can you come round and collect it tonight?"

"No problem, Jim."

"I feel that the only way to stop her would be if it was in your possession because you were the one who uncovered it. Completing the circle may stop her. After all, the deaths only occurred after you gave it to me. That may make a difference."

"I'm sorry to have dragged you into this, Jim."

"Don't blame yourself, someone would have found it eventually. If you hadn't you'd be oblivious to the curse, at least we know why these deaths are happening now, it's a shame that you literally stumbled upon the amulet, I wish it had stayed buried. The consequences of her being resurrected will be catastrophic unless we can find a way to defeat her."

Mark ended the call and told them all he was nipping out to Jim's and would be back soon. He drove to the house in Paddenham and Jim met him at the door. He was looking the worse for wear and his eyes were very red. Jim gave him the stone and wished him luck. Mark put the thing in his jacket pocket. He got back just as the pizzas were arriving and decided to tell them everything. About the curse, about his dreams and about the fog that seemed to follow him. The deaths, his meeting with Daly and his calls to Jim.

Ellie told them about her dreams and the incident in the copse near Marsham stones and Nat told of her experience the other night with the fog and the tapping on the window and Erika's fright in the car. It was all starting to piece together and they were all getting a bit scared. Mark wondered if it was time to tell Nat about her dad being presumed dead but decided to put it off again. After all, no news is good news as the saying went. There was still a chance he'd turn up. He hoped he'd never have to tell her and that the police will call her with some good news. They ate their pizza without too much of an appetite.

Ellie had another dream that night. She was back in the copse near the stones again. Fog was all around her. She could barely make out anything more than a couple of feet away. There was a crackling of twigs and branches like something was moving through them. She'd become soaking wet from the fog clinging to her clothing, she started to shiver. Was it the cold or the terrifying notion of something close by? She heard a faint whisper in the distance but it was hard to make out if there were any actual words. Panic gripped her and she tried to find a way out of the copse. In every direction she turned there was an obstacle, a tree or a bush, something to block her way. Her feet sank into the soft earth and mud clung to her shoes making her feet heavier by the second. She wanted to crouch and run her hands through the dark brown muck, wondered what it would taste like. The whisper was closer now but still indistinguishable. She wanted to make out what it said but that would mean whatever made the faint sound would have to come nearer to her. She trudged through the slime underfoot, getting nowhere it seemed. She sat down in the mud and picked up a handful. She heard the whisper again.

'Almost here, almost back!'

And again.
'Almost here, almost back!'

Ellie sat up, trying to breathe through the duvet that was stuffed into her mouth. She dragged it out and lay back down panting. Jack was oblivious to the disturbance like he had been to all the strange things that Ellie, Mark and Nat had experienced. What made him immune?

Wednesday May 6th

Breakfast was very subdued for Jack and Ellie that morning, none of the usual chatter about everyday, trivial things, each trying to make sense of what seemed to be happening. Jack refused to believe any of it, scoffing at the 'mere coincidence' of it all. Ellie gave him a black look and told him he'd believe if he'd seen what the rest of them had. Jack decided he wasn't in the mood for a fight and sat in a chair on the patio drinking his coffee alone. He needed to go into work today for a meeting with a big client and wanted to be relaxed for that. He sat there breathing in the cool morning air wondering if there wasn't something in it after all. Ellie was very level headed and didn't usually get that angry and she seemed scared, not just for herself but for Mark and Nat too. If it was all real then he wanted to help but didn't know how. He didn't believe in the supernatural but prided himself on his open mind. He walked back into the kitchen and apologised to Ellie and said he'd do all he could to help if she needed him. They hugged before Jack left for work.

Mark dropped Nat off at work as usual and then went on his way to his own. He was deep in thought as Stevie Ray Vaughan oozed from the stereo. *The Sky Is Crying* came on and that reminded Mark of Steve's funeral so he changed the CD to Sad Café. He went through the usual ritual of parking, buying his coffee and ascending in the cramped lift and got to the office and sat wearily in his swivel office chair. James was already there, ready to make the first call of the day. Mark liked him already even though they'd only worked together a few days. He'd settled in pretty easily to the work but Mark knew even an untrained monkey could sell these contracts if they found a mug on the other end of the phone. He preferred James to Paul by a long way and then felt guilty at the thought.

Lunchtime quickly came around and he walked out to his car to call Daly.

"Afternoon Inspector, are you busy?"

"I have a few minutes before I have to be in a meeting with the DCI, what did you find out?"

"Actually it may take longer than that. Can we meet in the pub again later?"

"No problem, I'll see you at six," said Daly and ended the call.

Mark texted Nat and said they would be meeting Daly later before they went home. She replied that it was fine as long as they didn't stay all night.

The afternoon dragged on, Mark wasn't having much luck with sales, his mind wasn't on top form and he was basically going through the motions. He kept going back to what he'd be telling Daly and how much the seasoned copper would believe.

Five o'clock on the dot Mark was on his way out to pick Nat up from work. He was waiting outside the jewellers when she came out looking exhausted. Mark drove back to the pub and Daly was already there and Mark wondered how many pints he'd had. He'd probably need them if what Mark had to say was true.

Mark paid for a fresh round, pints of Stella for Daly and himself and a half a pint of Strongbow cider for Nat, and they seated themselves in the same booth as before. It was a little busier than before so they tried to keep their voices down. Mark thought that if anyone heard their conversation the men in the white coats would arrive pretty soon.

"Okay, I'll just come right out and say it all then you can choose to believe this or not," said Mark.

"Fire away," Daly replied intently.

"This is going to sound mad but here goes and I'll try to make it brief. A couple of weeks ago I was out doing my usual walk across the field near where I used to live. On the walk I tripped over a tree root and saw something buried between the tubers and fished it out. It was a carved stone with runic symbols on it and a carved demon on the back. I took it home and cleaned it up a bit and took it to show my mum the next day. She put me in touch with Jim Anderson, a history professor and a bit of an expert on the supernatural and occult."

"He's the guy who gave you Brand's phone number?"

"That's him. After several calls and visits to his place and him calling his friends it turns out that the amulet was almost certainly owned by a healer in the fifth century called Kendra Watkin. Apparently she was wrongfully accused of witchcraft and the murder sacrifice of a child and burnt at the stake. Her remains were wrapped in chains and dumped in a pond on the land where I walk, close to where I found the amulet."

"With you so far," said Daly without any obvious expression.

"One of Jim's friends, a collector of Saxon stories and folklore, said the story passed down by word of mouth is that Watkin cast a spell to bring herself back from the dead and hid this stone amulet. Once found the demon depicted on the back would make five sacrifices to bring her back and for the sixth she'd be whole enough to do herself and complete the ritual. That woman was a powerful healer and apparently knew a lot of dark magic passed down to her by her grandmother. I'm not sure if you are aware but Jim's friend was the fifth victim two nights ago. Apparent suicide or heart failure from stuffing mud into his throat. His heart may have given up but it certainly wasn't suicide but that's how it will probably be recorded. It was the spell."

"So this 'demon' is causing people to kill themselves," said Daly.

"I thought there were only four victims so far," said Nat confused. "Brand, Paul, Steve and this archaeologist chap. Who have I missed, Mark?"

"We think your missing father may be one of the victims too," said Daly. "I'm sorry, I should have said something but officially he's still missing but given the connection to other three we have to assume..."

"He's dead?"

"Yes, we think so. I'm sure Mark has told you of the Marsham connection of the other three and your dad was born there too."

"Jim's friend was born in Marsham as well, he told me when I mentioned the pattern last night," added Mark.

"Why didn't you tell me?" Nat fixed Mark with an icy stare.

"I'm sorry Pixie, while he's officially missing there is still a chance they'll find him safe and I didn't want to tell you we thought he was dead and then amazingly he'd turn up in one piece. I couldn't do that to you."

Nat was only semi-placated by his explanation and was starting to come to terms with the fact that her dad was probably dead and they may never find him. She may not be able to say goodbye properly like Kim could with Steve.

"So," Mark said to Daly, "If all this is true it looks like we have five victims all born in Marsham, and I pray that Nat's dad isn't one, and that leaves one more and Watkin will commit that one herself. What do you think?"

"Interesting."

"Other people have had experiences too, my mum has had vivid dreams about the past and they seem to involve this Watkin, or at least someone like her. Nat heard tapping at the window the other night and her friend Erika had a weird experience going home after they both went out for a meal. We also think it was Watkin involved with the break-in. She wanted the amulet back. And there's the fog."

"Fog?"

"Yes, there always seems to be a fog lingering every time something happens. My mum was caught in a fog when she tried to get through the copse up at Marsham stones, Erika was trapped in her car by it in a country lane. There was fog outside mum's house when Nat heard her tapping and also when my mum got up in the night. She said she saw a shape in it that she put down to her imagination at the time. Then there was my experience when I had my accident. I was in the dell near my parent's house while walking and the dell filled with fog and I panicked and ripped my hand open on the barbed wire and sprinted across the field despite my back injury Then I passed out. I even saw it in a park near Oxford when we were away and I thought I saw a shape in the trees. I've even been getting a mysterious pain behind my eye which seems to be around the time these people are dying."

"It's all bloody mysterious, and guess what? I believe every word of it?"

"You do," said Mark amazed.

"I think I've told you before that I've seen and heard some very strange things over the years. Things you could never put in a police report or you'd soon find yourself demoted to a traffic cop with a reputation for being a right nutter. Not good for career progression, that's for sure. There is stuff out there that is just to hard to explain and most people wouldn't want to."

"That's a relief to know that it's not just in our heads, some collective hallucination."

"My most frightening case was in London. Squatters kept disappearing from a derelict house they had used for years. No trace of anyone after they went missing. Every time someone was reported as absent we looked into the place and found absolutely nothing. Normally when one of these vagrants disappeared we'd send a Plod to check the house out about two or three days afterwards because they just aren't a priority these days. They could have merely left of their own free will, shacked up with someone else or jumped in the Thames for all we knew, no one cares really. That sounds bad but investigating murders, rapes and these grooming gangs are far more important and any copper will tell you the same. Anyway, one of these squatters goes missing and it turns out to be the rebel son of an MP. The kid was trying to stick two fingers up at his dad and do his own thing, so obviously the brass wants to look good to the Government, and this MP in particular, who is a gobby little git who likes to tell the House how poor the crime figures are so I get sent out to have a look this time. I was there with Gibson, my sergeant at the time, and we'd questioned all the other squatters and they claimed to know nothing as usual. We went through the house and it was like we were on the X-Files, all pitch dark and torch beams flying about everywhere. We got to the cellar and saw this web stretching halfway across the room, looked creepy as hell. It was like a scene from that film *Arachnophobia* so we were on the lookout for a few hundred small spiders, probably harmless but we weren't taking chances, someone could have had a stash of Black Widows or something, you just never know. We heard a sound from the corner of the cellar and thought maybe the kid was hiding down there or off his head on drugs. Gibson went first and peered into a gap between some old cardboard boxes. I heard a scream thinking he'd woken the kid who had freaked out, possibly even having a bad trip. I wish to God it was. Gibson staggered back, most of his right arm missing, ripped away just above the elbow. What followed him was the biggest bloody spider I'd ever seen, or anyone had seen for that matter. The thorax was roughly three feet across and four long, the abdomen even bigger, the legs were different lengths and the longest had to be at least eight feet, maybe ten. It was all covered in a gingery blond fur or hair. There were four red eyes staring right at me. I froze for a second and the thing moved towards me. I managed to get my wits together and dragged Gibson up the cellar steps, he was in danger of bleeding out. We got to the car and I made him sit in the back seat and took my belt off to use as a tourniquet. I used the radio to call for a paramedic and made sure Gibson was a priority for them. I then called my DCI on my phone and said I needed him to authorise an armed unit sent to the address because some 'wild animal' had attacked Gibson. I was savvy enough not to say it was a giant spider with Gibson's arm hanging limply from it's fangs. The armed unit arrived like the bloody SAS and searched the place from top to bottom. They found nothing apart from a pool of blood on the floor. No sign of the spider. No sign of his arm either."

"Christ, I'd like to see that report."

"The official report says that Gibson was attacked by an animal of unknown origin, unidentifiable in the dark, which then escaped again, and the missing persons are still missing persons. One of those cases that are filed away and forgotten. One thing is for sure."

"What's that?" asked Mark.

"Gibson is crap at darts now." Daly's bellowed laugh drew several looks from the other drinkers. Even Mark had to smile at that despite his own problems. Gallows humour.

"So he survived then?"

"Yes, he works as a security guard in a supermarket now, poor bloke. Looked like an Albino with all that blood loss when they strapped him to a trolley and got him in the ambulance. Refused to have a false arm fitted too, I'd have probably done the same to be honest."

"So what the hell are we going to do about this?" asked Mark.

"We'll have another drink, that's what!"

Mark and Nat were spending a quiet night in trying to relax after the meeting with Daly. A light meal of frozen fish and chips cooked in their air fryer. Neither felt like preparing a proper meal and another takeaway was out of the question, they had to cut down to pay the bills. They were chilling out in front of the TV chatting about Nat's dad when the lights suddenly went out. Everything went pitch black.

"I doubt it's a power cut," Mark's voice sounded from the darkness. "Probably just a fuse tripping for some reason, stay where you are Pixie."

Mark fished his phone from his jeans pocket, turned on the flashlight function and made his way to the small airing cupboard in the hallway where he knew the fuse box was. He opened the cupboard door and looked to the bottom left, opened the cover of the grey fuse box and saw in the light from his phone that all the circuits had tripped. Mark thought that was pretty unusual. He pushed up the small red plastic levers one by one and heard various beeps from his electrical gadgets as they powered up again. The last switch turned the lights back on. Happy that it wasn't a power cut that could have lasted hours, if not all night, he got up and turned towards the living room. The leather two seater in front of the TV was empty, Nat's glass of wine tipped over creating a wet patch on the carpet.

"Very funny," groaned Mark. "You knocked over your glass trying to hide, lucky it's not red wine."

Mark decided to play the game just to humour her as she'd had bad news from Daly. He searched behind the sofa and the dining table. Nowhere else to hide there. Next the bedroom. He checked the wardrobes and under the bed. Nothing. He knew that she couldn't have got past him to the kitchen and bathroom while he was dealing with the fuses but checked them anyway. He even checked the airing cupboard on his way back to the front room.

"Nat?"

Silence.

"Okay, where are you?"

He even looked out of the window of the living room to check the deserted high street, barely illuminated by the orange street lamps. There was just no sign of her anywhere. He checked the bedroom again but realised it was pointless. He expected a little giggle to creep out of Nat the more frustrated he became but there was no sound at all.

"Come on Nat, joke's over. I wanted to relax this evening, not get stressed out."

Where the bloody hell is she? She has to be hiding somewhere, he thought. She didn't go out of the only entrance to the flat out onto the balcony, the alarm was set and would have triggered. It had it's own battery so wouldn't be affected by the power outage. She just couldn't have got out of the flat, even through the windows.

As he walked down the hallway again he brushed against his coat that was hanging on the rack near the door. He could feel an intense vibration coming from it. He put his hand in the pocket and gripped what he'd left inside. The amulet. Then he knew. He ran out the front door, slamming it, down the iron steps and sprinted for the Jag. He drove into the descending fog.

Nat regained consciousness, she seemed to be lying on the damp ground unable to move. Where was she? How did she get here. A shadow cast by the moon spread over her. She was in the stone circle but the fog mysteriously had not invaded the ring. A tall woman dressed in black stood there. She didn't seem entirely solid, her face fading in and out of focus.
"Who are you? Why am I here?" she cried, then: "Please don't hurt me!"
"You are here for a purpose... My purpose!"
"What purpose? What could you possibly want with me? Why?" Panic now starting to creep into her voice.
"My name is Kendra Watkin ... Mother Watkin to most. I was falsely accused and murdered and I WILL have my revenge. You will be the final sacrifice."
"NO! You can't. I've done nothing to you!" screamed Nat.
"Your ancestor did. He was the one who accused me of killing his daughter. I loved her as my own and on his testimony I was burnt and my remains dumped in a pond."
"It's not fair!" Nat cried like a small child denied.
"Do you think what happened to me was fair?" spat Watkin.
"You killed all those people, Steve and the rest ... My father!"
"They killed themselves under the influence of Anrok. The demon conjured when the amulet was found, he has always been bound to the stone. You, I'll kill myself. You are the most important one. Then it will be complete. I will be complete!"
Watkin moved her hand to the side and Nat fell into unconsciousness again.

Mark arrived at the stones near Marsham. He'd had to navigate through the dense fog and hoped he'd made it in time to save Nat. That was all he cared about even above his own safety or the consequences of Watkin returning to life permanently. He could feel the heat from the stone amulet in his hip pocket. The vibration had lessened the nearer he got to the stones in the car, replaced by a warm sensation. He peered into the fog for some clue where they were. He heard faint chanting in the distance and followed the sound. The fog had made the long grass wet and his trainers and the bottoms of his jeans were already soaked through. A shape began to form in the gloom. Should he rush in or use stealth instead of alerting her to his presence? The only weapon he had was the amulet. Would it be enough?

He decided that moving quietly under the cover of the fog and the stones was his best option. He had to get nearer to have any chance at all. The pulsating chant was getting louder but the fog was so thick it was impossible to judge just how far he was away from the stones and Watkin. He could see a faint blur of activity in the distance now but it was still hard to gauge the distance.

Then he felt like the life was being sucked from him, some force he didn't understand was draining the energy out of him. Did she sense him there or was it a residue of the power she possessed like the deadly radiation that spread after a nuclear explosion? He was getting weaker by the minute and he needed to act fast. He took a deep breath and bolted towards the sound with his last reserves of will and stamina.

He saw Nat lying on the sodden ground, her dark hair spreading from her pale looking face. She seemed either unconscious or in a deep trance. The black clad figure circled her and then stood still like she could have been formed from granite like the larger monoliths which dominated the clearing. Watkin slowly raised her hands in the air to draw on the power that was even more evident the closer he got to the circle. She was almost fully formed now and just needed one more sacrifice to become whole again and regain all of the power she had when she was alive, maybe even more. Mark was desperate to stop her. Not only for Nat but for the future victims of the witch. The undead army she could call upon would be unstoppable and would ensure she carried out her evil. She'd be even more determined now, spurred on by revenge.

Mark knew he had to stop the ceremonial murder, but how? The amulet was the key but how could he use it? The story Jim told alluded to the stones, but what were they supposed to do – come to life and attack the witch? That was too bloody ridiculous for words. The waves of power were emanating from Watkin and getting stronger. Think, he told himself. Bloody well think!

Watkin put a hand under her cloak and produced a long knife with a jagged, double sided blade and a gold hilt. She turned to stare at Mark and smiled, her partially unformed face shimmering in the moonlight. He knew he had very little time. Could he rush her and give his own life in order to be the sixth victim in the series of rituals? Would it stop her for now and save Nat? He didn't think so. The cycle would still be complete and so would Watkin. He must delay her attack on Nat and give himself more time to find a solution.

The stones! What the hell was it they could do to help?

Why not me?

He faced Watkin and shouted "Why not me, why wasn't I one of the six victims?"

"You found the amulet, you were protected, and so were your family, but when I am whole again nothing will protect any of you. No one will be safe from my retribution."

"Why do you need revenge? Everyone you ever knew has been dead and buried for over fifteen hundred years. Why can't you just stop?"

"All six where chosen because they are descendants of my tormentors. Their families remained local to the area. Some moved far away but I still found them. They will pay for those who accused me, convicted me, burnt me, I *will* have my revenge," hissed Watkin.

"Then why not stop at six, why carry on killing once you are resurrected?" pleaded Mark.

"BECAUSE I CAN!" screamed Watkin, spittle flying from her mouth. Can you imagine my spirit waiting for all these years? What I felt? What was left of my body rotting in that water for centuries? I was discarded and forgotten by the primitives of that village and their ancestors must pay. They knew I was innocent yet still carried out my murder. I will bring death or desolation to every single family still living here, the survivors will worship me if they want to live!"

"Don't take Nat, take someone else if you have to but leave her the hell alone!"

"She was always going to be the last of the six. She is from the direct bloodline of my accuser, Ware. My false accuser!"

Mark was out of ideas and almost out of time. Watkin took another step towards the prone Nat. The fog was thinning slightly and he could see the large granite slabs forming an outer ring around everything. Watkin was standing over Nat now, the deadly blade poised above her heart. The dull murmur in the air was getting louder, almost a drone now. Mark imagined that as soon as it abruptly ceased Watkin would plunge the knife down into Nat's chest and the ritual would be complete. Watkin would be mortal again and immensely powerful. To Mark's disbelief Nat raised her hands and took the knife from Watkin and turned it towards her own chest. She was being made to kill herself like all the others.

Mark could barely watch and knew it was hopeless. Shock started to take hold and he slowly backed away from the scene. He didn't know why. The situation was futile. Nat would soon be dead and he'd follow her along with thousands of others, maybe even millions. All the locals whose ancestry went back generations to the time when Watkin was executed would certainly die, maybe the rest of the population enslaved. He closed his eyes, refusing to watch the blade extinguish Nat's young life. His next step backed him into one of the giant stones. The amulet in his pocket was now so hot it was unbearable. He took it out and in a fit of rage turned and smashed it against the rock. There was a massive flash of pure white light and he was thrown several feet and everything went black again.

Some time later he felt a light caress on his forehead. Was he dead and an angel was soothing him? He tried to open his eyes and just saw a blur in front of him. Heaven would be boring if he was blind from that flash. Gradually his eyes began to focus and saw there was indeed an angel in front of him. It was Nat. At least they were together in the afterlife.

"You did it," whispered Nat, "I'm so proud of you."

"What, how?"

"Look."

She helped Mark stagger to his feet. His back felt like someone had hit him with a sledgehammer but managed to straighten up. Watkin was nowhere to be seen. Now there was an extra giant stone where she had been standing. Somehow the amulet had used her own magic to defeat the dark evil of the witch. He was still at a loss as to what actually happened but he *had* stopped her.

Mark limped down the path through the copse to the car as Nat continued to support him.

"Fancy driving?" he said to her. Mark never let Nat drive the Jag but after all they had been through he realised it was time they started to share a lot more things in future. *Baby You Can Drive My Car* by The Beatles played on the stereo as they drove off into the warm fog-free night. The fog reappeared inside the circle. Anrok looked at the additional granite block and knew the witch had failed. He cast his eyes down at his feet and he saw part of the shattered amulet, all that remained. Without it no one could control him again. He was free. Anrok stooped and picked it up, he now could generate his own power from the stones. He then disappeared into the gloom again, determined to return to this place once again.

Epilogue:

December

Nine months later in the Maldives, Mark emerged from the calm azure sea, the blazing sun on his back. He'd been snorkeling close to the coral breakwater that protected the island from any sharks that decided to come a bit close. He had a waterproof camera attached to his wrist by a rubber strap and had been taking underwater pictures of the many varieties of fish that swam around the intricate white coral reefs close to the shore. His new wife was lying on the beach on a towel reading a paperback version of Mark's bestselling book about the events in and around Marsham that previous terrifying spring.

Mark's dad had indeed walked Nat down the aisle as her father could not be located. The names had been changed in the book and sold as fiction because no one would believe the true story and as his publisher told him 'horror fiction sells' so he did what his publisher suggested and re-wrote his account as a horror story. Sales had been slow at first because he was unknown and then out of the blue one of the big broadsheet newspapers included his story in their book reviews and sales took off. Word of mouth helped enormously and it all snowballed from there including an interview on BBC Radio for a literary review show and then a production company paid him a quarter of a million for the rights to turn his book into a major film. He was fascinated as to who would be playing him in the film.

Nat smiled at him as he approached, still dripping from his excursion in the Indian Ocean. He had stayed close with Gerry Daly who was his best man at the wedding and as soon as Mark returned from honeymoon would be working with him on a new book about the giant spider.

"Any ideas for the next one?" she asked.

"One or two," he said and smiled.

He knew one thing for certain. He finally discovered what he wanted to do with his life.

Author's afterword:

Well, if you got this far then hopefully you enjoyed my first effort at writing a novel, or at least found it interesting. So please humour me for another couple of paragraphs if you will. Thomas J. Stone is a pen name. I make no apologies or excuses other than I'm a pretty private person and would like to remain anonymous for now. Maybe one day I'll be outed like Thad Beaumont in The Dark Half, hopefully without similar repercussions. Meanwhile I like the idea of slipping into someone else's shoes to create a world different from my own. This is the first time I've done any writing since boring old English lessons in a British Secondary Modern school in the late seventies. I have no doubt my grammar isn't perfect and probably mix tenses a few times but I'm looking to improve. So if you'd like to accompany me on my journey you are more than welcome.

Please feel free to comment on my Facebook (**Thomas J. Stone**) and Twitter (**@ThomasJStone3**) accounts. Let me know what you think and tell me if there are any characters you'd like to see return. Jim Anderson was originally supposed to be killed off but I took a shine to him and he will appear in the next book which is called **A Rip In Time**. I think Ellie could appear in her own story eventually too, I loved her recipes. Mark and Nat will also return at some point. Anrok has unfinished business.

I'd like to thank my friends for their encouragement, especially Julie, Phyllis and Erika (who pops up in the book but I wouldn't dare kill her off). They are also my official proof readers and provided a few improvements to the story too and I appreciate them to the moon and back.
Special thanks go to Sue Massey - an amazing artist who very kindly provided the cover for me. It was her work that Mark admired in the gallery. Check her out at https://www.deviantart.com/suemart and https://www.artistsandillustrators.co.uk/suemassey